Earl Grafton
AND THE Traitor

Earl Grafton

AND THE Traitor

ANGELA JOHNSON

Paperback ISBN: 978-1-955534-03-1

Hardcover ISBN: 978-1-955534-04-8

Edited by: Rachel Hathcock & Midnight Owl

Published by: Pemberley Publishing

For Cheri
Your love of reading inspired me at a young age. The only reason I
picked up a book to read was so I could be like my big sister.

Chapter One

Baxter Fernley, The Earl of Grafton, had no time for lightheartedness, laughter, or pleasure. At least, not since his father had passed away. Left with the responsibilities of his title, Baxter had an estate to run and a family to care for. His title and the expectations of earls before him haunted every decision he made. They had entrusted him with their legacy, and he would not forsake all they had passed down to future generations. Gone were leisurely hours where he could engage in a game of cards or physical activities with his brothers. He was now the earl, a magistrate, and protector of his family.

Baxter took his position in society seriously. As the magistrate over the local hamlets and towns near Primrose Hall, he was determined to handle all trials with fairness and within the confines of the law. He had purchased numerous law books, consulted with his younger brother, Fletcher, who happened to be a Barrister, and yet he still hadn't any idea how to handle the current trial before him.

Flames danced in the hearth warming the occupants in Baxter's den as they awaited his decision. The local constable, Mr. Craig, stood in the corner of the room like a statue while the young man before him struggled to stay upright. The boy's legs shook with a fear Baxter didn't understand because he'd never been in such a conundrum. The frivolities he'd indulged in during his youth had never led to lawlessness.

Baxter looked down at the young man before him. His youthful countenance was hidden by shadows of fear. The distress of his situation marked his face with dark circles under his eyes. He looked well over sixteen, but Baxter knew better. Even in his youthful state, the crime he was accused of was by all accounts punishable with death. Hanging to be exact. The last judgement Baxter wanted to make was to have the boy convicted of the crime, but all evidence was pointing to his guilt. "Mr. Donner, are you guilty of this crime?"

Visibly shaking, the boy looked down at the ground. Baxter patiently waited to see if he would find enough courage to admit his guilt. It couldn't be an easy confession given the severity of the penalty. As the boy's head came up, he looked Baxter in the eyes, showing a boldness no one in the room expected. "No, my lord."

"A falsehood, if ever I have heard one." Mr. James slammed his fist against the cushion of the couch as he looked away from his daughter. Miss Mary's head was buried in her hands as her shoulders shook and her mother patted her back.

Mr. Donner held his distraught wife as she crumbled in his embrace. Timothy was their only son, and any judgement against him would irreparably injure their family.

Holding the proceedings at Primrose Hall was Baxter's way of keeping the town out of the courtroom. Even with this effort, Baxter knew word would spread through every parlor in town. Supper conversation would involve retellings of the entire event, even if the information was fabricated. "Please, calm yourselves. Mr. Donner," Baxter said looking at the boy. "May I call you Timothy?"

"Yes, my lord."

"Timothy, what can you tell me about your acquaintance with Miss Mary James?"

Mr. James stepped forward and pushed Timothy aside. Standing before Baxter, Mr. James pulled everyone's attention off the alleged criminal. "What does this accomplish? My daughter is in fear for her life due to this vagrant. His continued lies will only increase her worry. She spends her nights in tears and does not sleep."

Baxter refused to pronounce judgement upon anyone without knowing the full truth of a situation, and he wasn't about to cower to a man like Mr. James. James may have money and land, but he wasn't the magistrate, nor was he on the same social level as Baxter. As an earl and magistrate, Baxter was the voice of law and reason within his earldom.

"Mr. James, your daughter will be given a chance to speak. At this moment, we will hear from Timothy Donner." Baxter glared at Mr. James until he backed away and took a seat next to his wife. When he was satisfied, Baxter turned back to the boy and encouraged him to speak with a kind nod of his head and a half smile.

Timothy plunged his hands into the pockets of his trousers and nervously swayed from left to right as he started his tale. "I was working at the livery when Mr. James and Miss Mary stopped in with a lame horse. They'd been out riding, and the gelding threw a shoe." Timothy peeked out of the corner of his eye toward his father and with a gentle nod, the man extended support to his son.

Emotions welled up inside as Baxter considered the distress of the Donner family. If their son was innocent, Baxter wanted to find a way to save him from the cruelty of conviction. Baxter knew the Donner family well. They were tenants of the estate and had been at Primrose Hall often working on carriage axles and other items in the livery. The accusation against the boy had been shocking and confusing for Baxter. He'd always seen Timothy as a good soul.

Timothy's lips tightened for only a second, but it was enough to show further strain and desperation in his features. As he continued speaking, he focused his eyes on Baxter's desk. "I thought Miss Mary was the handsomest chit I'd ever laid eyes upon."

With this confession, Mr. James burst from his seat and placed his hand firmly on Timothy's shoulder. Pulling the boy around, Mr. James glared down upon the young man. "You will never claim to have laid eyes upon my daughter again." With black shadows below his eyes, Mr. James looked to be in as much stress as the other family. No one would leave this trial a victor. No matter the outcome, one family would lose, and the personal torture would continue. "My lord, can you not compel this young man to admit his guilt? Please, exercise the full extent of the law upon him and bring peace to my family."

Baxter understood Mr. James's outburst. The confession had been bold, but for the sake of justice, the testimony needed to continue. But there was no reason to subject the women to further testimony. Their delicate sensibilities needn't be exposed to such details. "Mr. James, if you would prefer Miss Mary wait in the parlor with my mother, we can continue the trial. Your wife should go as well." Turning to the other woman in the room, he held Mr. Donner's attention. "If Mrs. Donner would prefer to leave, we will wait until she is settled in the parlor."

They waited as Mrs. James and Mary exited the den, but Mrs. Donner refused to leave her son. When the chambers were settled and filled with the tense breathing of those left, Baxter motioned with a wave of his hand for the proceedings to continue. Baxter had hoped this would prove an easier task, but the law was never simple and young love was even more difficult to handle.

Timothy hesitated and looked back to the top of the desk. "I admit to walking out to the James's estate in hopes of a simple glance upon her curly blond hair. I'd never seen soft fine hair before. Miss Mary noticed I was lingering nearby, and we became friends. We didn't mean to fall in love."

"This is an outrage!" Mr. James bellowed toward Baxter, his face turning a deep red.

Baxter was known for his patient manners, but Mr. James had

overextended Baxter's resolve. They would never come to a resolution if Mr. James continued to interrupt the testimony. "Mr. James, do you need to sit in the parlor with my mother as well?"

Mr. James cleared his throat and retook his seat. He straightened his jacket and fiddled with his cravat, his shoulders slumped with embarrassment. "That will not be necessary, my lord. I do apologize for my outburst."

"I do not think anyone in this room will fault you for your concern over Miss Mary. But we must continue the testimony if a judgement is to be made." Baxter again waited until everyone looked settled, and then he gave Timothy the license to continue speaking.

"I know it is wrong to love a girl above my social standing, but I cannot still the aching in my heart when I think of her. When Papa found out about my wanderings, he put a stop to them, and I never visited the James Estate again. I promise, my lord."

"What about the letter, Timothy? Did you write it?" Baxter kept his voice calm. He wanted the boy to know he was safe. It wouldn't do any good for him to frighten Timothy with accusations and harsh words.

Timothy's eyes were filled with fear and his skin pulled tight on his face, exposing the outline of his cheekbone. Either the boy hadn't been able to eat due to his fear, or he was suffering from malnutrition. Timothy boldly met Baxter's gaze. "No, I didn't."

Mr. James's agreement to silence didn't last as long as Baxter had hoped. He jumped to his feet again and wagged a finger at Timothy. "Lord Grafton, you cannot trust the impoverished to tell the truth. He has declared himself. His feelings for my daughter are not right, given he is a lower-class citizen."

"Mr. James, we will hear from your daughter before I retire to consider each of the testimonies."

"She has nothing to say, other than she is fearful for her life."

"Very well." Baxter looked to the constable. "You will ensure

Timothy's safe return to his home for the evening? I will consider my verdict and have a response by morning."

As Baxter spent the evening reviewing his notes and the threatening letter Miss Mary James had received three days previously, Baxter wondered why the boy would have threatened the girl. He claimed to be in love. It also made no sense for him to have signed his name at the bottom of the letter. The entire situation didn't sit right with him, and he worried it would take more than one evening to make a judgement.

Chapter Two

Briar Kensington pulled the extra cape layer of her cloak tightly around her body as she stepped off the gangway, displaying a confidence she didn't feel. The wind blew straight through her pelisse and bonnet, causing gooseflesh to bubble over her entire body. Searching for a grandfather she'd never met, Briar noticed the visible puff of air escaping as she breathed.

"Mr. Kensington paid us to accompany you to port. We are not required to wait and catch our deaths in this weather." Mr. Holstead pursed his lips as he peered down at her, his spectacles on the edge of his nose. "I do hope he does not leave you waiting long."

"Mr. Holstead, we cannot leave this young woman unprotected. It would do little good to have stayed by her side through the entire voyage only to allow her to fall into ruin now." Mrs. Holstead made a spectacle of herself as she peered at passing travelers, expecting to find one or more with nefarious intentions. She was a kind woman, a bit eccentric and strict, but Briar had considered her close to a grandmother during the crossing from Boston to England. The only part of the trip she could truly complain about was the bothersome need for the woman to correct and remind her husband on their duty. Her grandfather had paid them handsomely for the escort, and Mr. Holstead had complained abundantly.

It was hard not to be frightened as she considered her situation. Her life had forever changed the moment her parents died. Instead of finding comfort in her own home and country, she'd sailed to her father's homeland to become a burden on the only relative who wanted her.

"Are you Miss Briar Kensington?"

The man was far too young to be her grandfather, but he was the only person looking for her. "Yes, and you are?"

"My name is Fred. I'm a footman at Kensington Park. Mr. Kensington is waiting for you in his carriage."

She didn't have any reason not to believe the cheerful young man, and so Briar embraced Mrs. Holstead while thanking the couple for their kindness. She allowed Fred to lead her through the crowds of people, fully trusting he would take her to her grandfather. The dockyard was filled with a contrast of people bundled in greatcoats and street urchins, half-dressed, who likely hadn't seen a tub of water for likely many years, selling their daily catch. Briar stepped with care to ensure the shoes hems of her skirts didn't fall prey to the fish guts and entrails littering the stained cobblestones. The distraction of so much energy around her kept her nerves from overreacting. She was terribly nervous, but she didn't need anyone to know that.

As she approached a large traveling carriage emblazoned with an elaborate letter K, the Kensington family crest, Briar was thankful Fred had led her to the correct place. Her grandfather exited the carriage upon her arrival, and she instantly recognized him as family for he was an elderly version of her father. She hoped he would be the kind man she expected. With a curtsey, Briar took one last chance to calm her nerves before making a complete spectacle of herself. "Grandfather, thank you for everything you have done to bring me to England." In her heart she wasn't truly thankful, but saying as much would be unkind. She missed Boston and the familiarity of her home and friends. The voyage to England had been difficult, cold, and lonely, even with her maid and Mr. and Mrs. Holstead for company.

"I am so pleased you arrived safely. I want to hear everything about your journey, and I want to know you better. We have a long trip back to Kensington Park, and it will give us time to become acquainted."

Briar nodded. She was thankful her grandfather wasn't anything like the stuffy British men who'd dined at her home throughout the years. She'd imagined England and her grandfather much differently. But Mr. George Kensington was a tall, handsome, and kind man, exactly as her father had been.

A little of the trepidation she'd felt since setting sail eased, and Briar decided she would make the best out of her circumstances. She would miss walking along the cobbled stones of history, roads on which George Washington had led the Continental Army to victory. She would never again look up at the steeple on the North Church to see the lanterns and remember the bravery borne by all the colonists as they'd joined together to fight against the tyrannical King George III. She was now living in King George's country and under his rule.

"Briar, I know you miss your friends and your home. But I believe England has much to offer."

Her grandfather was correct. She did miss her home, and it was difficult to imagine a new life away from all she held dear. Her father had regaled her with stories of the countryside where he'd grown up, and she knew there was much to be appreciated about this place. But as she had arrived only moments before, she had yet to discover any of its sources of entertainment.

Briar knew from the kindness in her grandfather's eyes that she could share the concerns of her heart. "Do you think people will accept me?"

"You are a Kensington, my dear girl. You will be the center of

Yorkshire Society for months, and you will be begging for me to decline invitations before long."

Briar admired her grandfather's ability to put her at ease. With a heated brick at her feet and a pile of wool blankets covering her body, she wasn't cold. The trip to Yorkshire was bumpy, but her grandfather's carriage was of the best quality, and she was only jostled when the wheel hit a hole in the road. As they neared Kensington Park, Briar made a plan to take each day as it came, and she hoped over time, the longing for her real home and her parents would go away.

Chapter Three

Timothy Donner's trial weighed heavily on Baxter's mind as he went through the motions of eating supper and then spending the evening with his family in the drawing room. His brothers were at Primrose Hall for the winter break in the season. He didn't mind their chatter, especially with Gigi.

Gigi was their family term of endearment for the Dowager Countess of Grafton, their mother. When his mind was focused on the duties of his estate, it was easy for him to forget about conversation. This made his brothers the perfect houseguests because they didn't need him to pay attention.

Baxter closed his eyes, remembering the fear in Timothy's shaking legs as he swayed side to side. The boy was thin from malnutrition, which bothered Baxter. He knew the Donners didn't have many earthly possessions, but they should possess the wherewithal to feed their children.

"Baxter, what has you so preoccupied? You have not spoken a word all evening." Gigi's motherly concern pulled Baxter out of his thoughts. It wasn't surprising that she'd noticed his silence. She had seven sons, yet somehow managed to keep watch over all of them without fail.

"My mind is troubled with the Donner boy's trial. I am admittedly concerned." Baxter looked to his mother. Could she offer the advice he needed? His father would've known exactly what to do. No hesitation. No delay. The previous earl would have settled the entire matter before the winter sun had set.

"The entire ordeal weighs upon you. Your face is worn, making you look much older than your thirty years." Gigi gave him a sympathetic smile, which unfortunately didn't ease the heaviness pressing upon Baxter's chest.

"The boy is adamant that he is in love with the girl and that he did not write the threatening letter. How can I decide between these arguments? I cannot say he did or did not write the words."

Gilbert leaned forward, placing his elbows upon his legs, which told Baxter he was considering how to share his thoughts. As the local vicar, Gilbert could be considered the only Fernley brother more ponderous than Baxter. Everyone waited as the clock on the mantle ticked away, marking the seconds before he finally spoke. "I know the Donner family well. Timothy is a good boy. He would not have done such an egregious act. As the vicar, I will vouch for him."

It might not have sounded like much to anyone outside their family, but Gilbert's determination to defend the boy was the confirmation Baxter needed to make his final decision. But how did he tell Mr. James he was siding with the Donner boy? And who was the person responsible for the letter? If Mary James was in danger, as the magistrate, Baxter needed to ensure her safety.

"I agree with Gil," Phineas said. No one expected anything less. Phineas and Gilbert were twins, Phineas being the eldest by thirty seconds. "I was speaking to Maggie Donner this morning. She's a sweet little girl. She told me her older brother and father go without supper most nights so their mother and the girls have enough."

The Donner's financial situation was one more concern to add to his list of issues for the estate. As the protector of these people, he had a duty to them. "Mother, will you arrange to take charity baskets to the Donner family for the next few months? I will find a way to increase Mr. Donner's stipend without causing him any embarrassment."

"I would be happy to do so. But your immediate problem is the trial. How will you resolve Mr. James's concern over his daughter's welfare?"

Baxter shook his head and pursed his lips in concentration. It was a difficult situation to be in, and he'd prefer to have his father available for advice. "If any of you can shed some wisdom, I will listen. I see no way of resolving the situation without making one of the families suffer."

Gil scooted back against the sofa and crossed his leg. "In the Bible, when King Solomon was faced with a difficult question of parentage between two arguing women, he demanded a sword be brought, and when he declared the child should be cut in two, it resolved the situation without delay. The mother of the babe refused to allow her child to suffer death, which told King Solomon which of the ladies was telling the truth."

Baxter knew the story well. He'd not only heard it in sermons since he was a boy, but their governess had impressed scriptural reading upon them at a young age. "I have not the wisdom of Solomon, and a sword will do me no good."

Gil smiled and nodded his understanding. "I agree, but have you considered speaking with Miss Mary James? I noticed she was not called back into the den this morning."

"Mr. James claimed she had nothing to add."

"Just as I said I would vouch for Timothy, I will share what I know of Mary James. She has a good heart and she tries hard to be a proper girl, but she enjoys chaos and needs constant confirmation of her parent's undying devotion."

Baxter steepled his fingers under his chin as he considered every-thing Gilbert said. "You believe Mary is responsible for the letter?"

"I do." Gilbert's unwavering answer caused a stir amongst the family. It was obvious from the tenuous conversations that no one was certain what to believe.

Gigi put her hand over her heart. The shock of such an allegation would be disastrous to their family if Gilbert were wrong and Baxter followed the advice. Gigi looked to Gilbert. "Do you have anyway of proving this?"

"Unfortunately, I cannot think of anything."

Baxter chuckled as he rested his head against the back of the chair. There was a simple way to resolve the issue, one he should have realized long before that moment.

"I hope this means you have come to a solution," Gigi said.

"Yes, I have. I will ask Miss James and Mr. Donner to each write a few of the words on a sheet of paper. I will then compare the handwriting and see if there is any way of determining the culprit."

"A very reasonable solution." Gil nodded his approval.

It did make sense, and it had been the Biblical story of King Solomon that had helped him think through the process. Baxter looked to his wise younger brother. "Gil, you saw the solution and waited for me to figure it out. Thank you."

"I do not know what makes you think I had a solution. I merely helped you by babbling on about scripture. I always find the word of God helps me think through my troubles."

"If this proves a sufficient way of determining who wrote that letter, I will step down from my position as magistrate and convince anyone who will listen to name you my successor."

Gilbert shook his head without any hesitation. "No, brother, my position as vicar is all-consuming. I do not think I could be magistrate."

"A pity," Baxter said, and he meant it. His younger brother was much wiser than he, and Gilbert was astute and perfectly capable of performing the duty of magistrate.

STANDING IN FRONT OF TIMOTHY AND MARY SHOULDN'T have made his palms sweat, but his gloves uncomfortably suctioned to his hands. The quills scratched against each sheet as the writer recorded the words Baxter spoke. "Kill." Positioned on each side of the desk with a cloth separator held up by Mr. James and Mr. Donner, neither could see the nuances of the other's handwriting. "Lovely."

As he said the words, Baxter thought of King Solomon and his father. Both were wise. Both would have discovered a more efficient way of solving this trial. And both were dead, making it impossible for them to offer advice.

"You may place your writing instruments on the table. You may each take a seat next to your mother while I decide on a solution to this mystery."

If neither of the handwriting samples matched the original letter, Baxter would have to start at the beginning. The constable would have to continue a nightly watch on the James Estate while everyone in town hoped the culprit could be located. A threat against one person was tantamount to threatening the entire community.

"This was a complete waste of my afternoon." Mr. James threw his end of the cloth separator at Mr. Donner, and then he moved over to the sofa and sat next to his wife. "What purpose was there in having my daughter engage in this activity?"

Baxter motioned for Mr. Donner to place the cloth on the table. There wasn't any need for the man to stay standing when Mr. James was determined to sit. Baxter didn't speak until he had examined both writing samples and made a comparison to the original letter.

Although she'd tried to hide the swirl on the letter *y*, and a telling loop on the letter *l*, Baxter was certain the handwriting of Miss Mary matched that of the letter. Timothy's handwriting was small and sloppy with multiple misspellings. It was obvious to anyone with sense the boy hadn't written the letter.

"Mr. James, I do not think your daughter has need to fear for her life." Baxter held the writing samples out, allowing the parents and the constable to see how he'd arrived at the conclusion. "Mr. Donner is innocent of all charges against him. He is free to go home without an escort from the law."

"Innocent?" Mr. James screeched. "How can you claim so when he presumed to declare himself? My daughter's reputation hinges on the outcome of this trial."

Baxter had yet to settle a penalty on Miss Mary for writing the letter, and he had been prepared to ignore Timothy's claim of love, but Mr. James wasn't likely to allow him to forget about the declaration. "Miss Mary, can you tell us what prompted you to write the letter?"

Mr. James scoffed while protectively placing his hand on Mary's arm. "You have no right to ask my daughter such a question."

Baxter had grown weary of the man's incessant need to be impertinent. "Mr. James, you will refrain from interrupting the court proceedings, or you will be escorted out of these chambers." Turning back to Mary, he encouraged her to speak.

Mary whispered at first, but her voice gained in strength as she gathered courage. "Timothy and I would meet in the fields each day and talk, until Mr. Donner made him stop visiting. I love Timothy, and I hoped the letter would be a punishment for ignoring me."

Baxter was shocked at the admission. He hadn't expected Mary to admit her guilt so readily. With her lips pursed in defiance, Baxter noted her lack of regret. The entire debacle was deeply concerning, but her inability to see her error in judgement sent a chill through Baxter's body. The girl needed to understand the penalty she'd nearly invoked upon the boy she claimed to love. "Were you prepared for the full extent of the law to be pronounced upon Timothy?"

"I thought he would be brought before the court and punished. I hoped you would make him work off the debt on our farm." Mary's ignorant plea left Baxter ill at ease.

He needed to help the girl understand the consequences of her actions, and it would have to be done by pronouncing a judgement upon her. She was the guilty party, and she deserved to be punished. "Miss Mary James, having found you guilty of the inadvisable behavior of lying to the court and bearing false witness against another person, your penalty will be six months of labor in the local workhouse."

Mr. James stood up and shook his head. "No. No. No." The crazed desperation of his eyes made Baxter more convinced a punishment must be given. "Mary is young and will learn from her mistakes. She does not deserve to have her reputation suffer from manual labor. I suggest we come to a monetary arrangement. What would you have me pay Mr. Donner so this entire debacle can be forgotten?"

Baxter wanted to deny Mr. James, until his eyes fell upon Timothy. His hollow cheeks and sunken eyes were a stark reminder of the malnutrition the boy had suffered. Money would be of greater value to the Donner family than the few chores Miss Mary would perform in a workhouse. It needed to be a hefty price, since the penalty for Timothy would have been death by hanging. "If you would prefer to settle your daughter's debt, you will pay Mr. Donner five hundred pounds."

Mr. James backed away from his wife and daughter, his face contorted in outrage. A gasp of surprise sounded on the opposite side of the room, and Baxter turned to see Mrs. Donner with her hand over her mouth, eyes wide in shock as she clung to her son. As everyone slowly digested Baxter's words, their eyes all rested upon him. Baxter wouldn't back down. Either James would pay the fee, or his daughter would spend six months at the workhouse.

"One hundred pounds," James said in an effort of negotiating.

"Six hundred pounds," Baxter replied.

"Not a pound more than two hundred."

Baxter could negotiate until supper was served. He wasn't about to give up. "One thousand pounds, or six months at the workhouse." As magistrate, his ruling stood, but Baxter enjoyed seeing Mr. James's face turn bright red with frustration.

"Fine. I will send a payment of five hundred pounds to Mr. Donner."

Baxter quirked an eyebrow in Mr. James's direction. "I do believe we were up to one thousand pounds. I will expect the payment to be sent to Primrose Hall by fourteen hundred hours tomorrow, or your daughter will report to the workhouse on Monday morning."

As Mr. and Mrs. James left, their daughter forced out the door by both parents pulling her along, Baxter turned back to Mr. and Mrs. Donner. "I will expect to see you, Mr. Donner, tomorrow at fourteen hundred hours as well."

Nervously clutching his hands, Mr. Donner looked to the floor avoiding Baxter's gaze. "My lord, the amount is too dear."

Baxter knew Mr. Donner could work every day for the rest of his life and never earn one thousand pounds. The amount must seem terribly overwhelming, and he understood the man's reservations on accepting such a large sum. "If your son had been found guilty, we would currently be discussing a burial plot. I will hear no more arguments on the size of the settlement."

Baxter waited until he was alone in his office before resting his head on the desk in utter appreciation of the outcome. The silence in the room was punctuated by the ticking of a clock and the crackling of the fire. Both noises were comforting. As he slowly let out a long sigh, he allowed the tension in his body to release. He didn't have to condemn a boy to death, and he could rest knowing the Donner family had enough money to keep food on the table without fear of going hungry.

Deep down, he knew that although he'd found a solution to this issue, he still wasn't wise like King Solomon or his father, but he was learning how to be a leader, and this situation couldn't have ended better.

Chapter Four

Briar liked Kensington Park, but the lack of friends made it boring. Her days were filled with embroidery and books. She hated embroidery, enjoyed books, but too much of a good thing led to boredom. The library at Kensington Park was plentiful if one wanted to read the history of wars. But deep in the corner of the room, an area she considered to be a nook, she had found a pleasant assortment of fictional literature. Three shelves were stuffed tight with titles merely purchased for the entertainment they provided.

Since arriving at her grandfather's home, she'd discovered he wasn't accustomed to having visitors, and therefore he often forgot she was in the house until meals. Her grandfather was a merchant, and his business needed attention. She knew her father had been a part of the business. Now that her father was gone, her grandfather was back to running the entire company, and Briar was left to her own devices.

Bundled in spencer, a pelisse, a shawl, bonnet, and boots, Briar stood in a snow-filled garden wondering if spring would ever come. She hadn't seen the sun since arriving in Yorkshire and she missed the way light sparkled like glass on snowflakes, at least it had done as much when she'd been in Boston. Unfortunately, since her arrival in England the sky had been overcast, leaving the snow dull. Briar meandered along the stone path, taking care not to slip on the icy cobblestones. As she walked to the side of the house, she was surprised to find her grandfather exiting the double doors that led to his study.

"Briar, I am happy to see you are taking the air. May I join you?"

Nodding in agreement, Briar accepted his outstretched arm. "Are you finished with business today?"

"No, but I needed a break from the rigors of accounting."

"Grandfather, may I inquire as to why you prefer to run the business? Could you not hire a manager to take my father's position? If accounting is strenuous, would it not be wise to find someone who could do the work for you?"

"I am a self-made man. As a merchant, I have always been part of the daily business decisions. Perhaps one day I will find someone to trust as much as I did my son, but for now, I must accept the responsibility."

This worried Briar. Her father had traveled most of the year for this company. Would her grandfather take on that responsibility as well? "Is there anything I can do to assist you in your work?"

"No, my dear. You are to be free of such worries. I will not have your reputation tarnished by people believing you have taken a profession."

Reputations were delicate in England. They were in Boston as well, but it was different. No one would have cared if she helped balance the books for her father. She never had, for she was proficient with neither mathematics nor accounting, but she liked to think she could learn and be helpful. In England, she was supposed to spend her days in womanly tasks, which amounted to a lot of nothing. Kensington Park ran smoothly under the direction of the housekeeper.

"What will happen to me when you need to travel?" Ever since her parents had died, her life had been upended, and she knew little of what to expect for her future. Her chest tightened with concern. Each time she thought about the unknown aspects of her life, the grip of fear clenched her heart.

"I have not yet decided what to do. I hope to not have to leave Kensington Park until you have married."

"Married?" She tried not to sound too shocked, but she hadn't even considered finding a husband since leaving the states. On the verge of panicking, Briar spoke rapidly. "I do not know anyone in England besides you and the staff at Kensington Park. Whom am I supposed to marry? How will I be a wife when I have yet to find my place in England?"

Her grandfather laughed and patted her arm. "Do not be so frightened. I have made a list of my acquaintances. I am certain one of these men will do for you."

Briar had to put a stop to the nonsensical conversation. She needed to let her grandfather know she was determined to marry a man of her choosing. Gathering her courage and hoping to sound diplomatic instead of ungrateful, Briar stopped walking and looked to the man who had taken her in when there were no other options. The kindness in his eyes left her unsettled as she momentarily thought of her father. He'd had the same softness and wrinkles. Three wrinkles stretched from the corners of both her grandfather's eyes and melted into his hairline. "Grandfather, I dare not consider marriage to one of your friends without a proper introduction." It hadn't come out the way she'd hoped. She sounded complicit in his decision to marry her off.

"I understand, my dear. There is nothing to worry about. Before the month is out, there will be plenty of opportunities for meeting young men. In fact, Lord Grafton has a house full of eligible bachelors. One of the Mr. Fernleys should do for you."

"Oh?" Briar didn't stop concern from entering her voice this time. Would she find herself married to a Mr. Fernley so soon? Were they the kind of men who wanted an arranged marriage? "How will you go about arranging the situation?"

"Upon an introduction, I will determine which man will suit you best. You are a very pretty young lady, and I have no doubt the men in our town will fill our morning room before long." Her grandfather patted her hand. "I suspect you will flutter around them as well. Most women cannot contain themselves around our neighbors."

Unwanted excitement entered her heart with this statement, but before she allowed herself to dream of courtship and romance, she had to know if she'd understood correctly. "You will allow me to make the decision of which man I am to marry?"

Her grandfather chuckled. "I hope you were not imagining a scenario where I forced you into a match. I could never do such a detestable thing."

The tight grip on her heart loosened as she realized her grandfather was not attempting to force her into an unwanted marriage. He'd kept all his promises to her since the day his first letter had arrived after her parents' deaths, and so she had every reason to believe he would continue to be honorable. She didn't want to admit her folly, but honesty was always best. She nodded and laughed at the absurdity of her fears. She could trust her grandfather. She almost let the entire conversation die out until she remembered he would have to travel.

"What if you have to leave Kensington Park on business and I have not found a husband?" Briar waited for his answer while he led her back toward the house. As they entered through the doors to his den, the warmth of the fire hit her face and a chill rushed through her body.

"I will make arrangements for you to stay with a neighbor. You will not be left alone."

Satisfied with his answer, Briar allowed her grandfather to escort her into the parlor, where she spent the afternoon working on embroidering a handkerchief. In her loneliness, she found herself daydreaming about Boston, tea with friends, walks along the harbor, and the smell of sea salt in the wind. Boston was everything England had yet to be. She needed to find a way to enjoy her new home.

When she'd been a little girl, her father had described Kensington Park to her. She'd longed to visit and see the spacious rooms with high ceilings. He'd described the extensive grounds with rose gardens and an apple orchard. She had yet to see roses and apples, but his descriptions of the house had been perfect. She was satisfied with almost everything, but she missed the harbor and walks along the ocean.

"Miss Kensington." Parker stood next to her holding out a silver tray with a cream-colored card in the middle. "You have a guest."

"I do not know anyone in England. Are you certain the person is here to visit me?"

"Yes, miss. I told her you were at home but had yet to set visiting hours."

"Who is it?" Briar was confused. Her grandfather hadn't mentioned any visitors, and it was late in the day. She was certain most people visited during set hours, as Parker had kindly reminded her when he'd mentioned that she had not yet agreed to a schedule. Briar looked expectantly at Parker and then noticed he was pointing at the card. "I am sorry, Parker." She looked at the clock and noticed it was two o'clock in the afternoon. "I will accept visitors each day between the hours of eleven and three."

"Very well, miss. And there is no need to apologize to me." Parker kindly whispered the admonishment.

She'd stumbled again. "Oh goodness!" Briar took the card and read the name. "Lady Grafton? Are you certain she asked for me and not my grandfather?"

"She is in the morning room."

Briar looked to Parker, an eyebrow raised in question. "It is no longer morning. Would it be better to visit in an afternoon room?"

Parker's lips twitched as he held back a smile. "Unfortunately, we do not have an afternoon room, but I will suggest it to your grandfather."

Briar gave Parker her brightest smile and left him so she could visit with her guest. She hoped this meeting would be the start of a good impression, as her grandfather had mentioned Lady Grafton's unmarried sons earlier.

Chapter Five

Baxter enjoyed having his family at Primrose Hall. Since his father's death, it wasn't often the entire family was together, and Baxter often found the halls of their home to be dreary and empty of joy without everyone. He understood they had obligations, most of them in London, but home was home, and Baxter believed every one of them still belonged in Yorkshire.

Oliver sat at the pianoforte, a flute in his hand and blank sheets of parchment ready for his next musical creation. Phineas preferred a place in the corner as he pored over a book about Egyptian artifacts with a magnifying glass and his spectacles. Of all his brothers, Baxter was most concerned about Phineas. His head was in the clouds searching for adventure, and Baxter hoped to find a way to cure him of the desire. Cornelius and Gilbert sat near the fire speaking in low tones. From the serious concentrated gestures and occasional frowns, he knew they were in a deep discussion on the theologies of war and faith. Archibald sat in the window box, pen and parchment poised for writing, yet his page sat blank as he stared out at the darkening snowy landscape, and Fletcher looked to be sleeping next to Gigi. It had been a long day, and Baxter expected a restful night as each pursued their different interests.

"Baxter, are you certain you do not mind hosting a few social functions over the next month?"

"Mother, I still consider this your home. You are free to do as you wish." As the Earl of Grafton, the estate belonged to him, but that didn't mean he'd ever refuse his mother entertainment. Gigi remained in the large home; he'd requested she stay because he was yet unmarried, which made the dowager house unnecessary. There was also a small part of him that believed if she was still in the home, where she and his father had raised a brood of seven sons, it would mean his father was simply away attending to the affairs of the title. It had been such a short time since his father had passed, there was no reason to change everything about the estate.

"I plan to invite the neighborhood to celebrate the arrival of Mr. Kensington's granddaughter. She's been in Yorkshire for a fortnight, and we have yet to meet her at a party."

Baxter knew Gigi had paid a call to the newest addition of the neighborhood. She'd spoken of little else since meeting the young lady. "Do as you wish."

"You might want to make one night a musical evening," Oliver said. "I have heard dancing in America is different than we are accustomed to."

Gigi smiled indulgently. "Whatever gave you such a silly notion, Oliver?"

Oliver looked up from the piano where he was composing a tune. "Everyone in Yorkshire has discussed Miss Kensington, Gigi. They all worry she will be out of sorts if invited to a ball."

"How silly." Gigi looked to Baxter, expectation written on her face. "You will be a gracious host and offer your arm to Miss Kensington. Two dances should be sufficient, and I expect one of them to be the supper dance."

"Two dances?" Baxter asked. He'd never chosen to dance with a woman twice in one evening. It was the best way to avoid gossip. As heir to an earldom, he didn't need the commotion of expectations built into a second dance. Now, as a man who had come into his inheritance, the hopes and dreams of debutantes and their mothers frightened him far worse than they had in the past. "I should think one dance would be sufficient."

Gigi smiled, more to herself than to him. Baxter wondered what could be going through her mind as her lips stayed locked in a tight conspiratorial smile. As she studied his face, he pulled out the book he'd brought to the drawing room in hopes that he could avoid her knowing gaze. There was nothing for her to know, for he hadn't been introduced to Miss Kensington. Yet, her continued staring made him nervous.

"Dearest, I think it would be nice to have Miss Kensington over for supper a few nights each month. I am drawn to her as a mother is to a daughter."

"Excuse me?" Baxter asked the question, and he wasn't surprised when each of his brothers stopped their various tasks to listen. Even Fletcher stirred from his nap and straightened his posture in confusion.

"I only mean to say the poor girl has lost both her parents and was passed between friends and distant relatives in the states before Mr. Kensington was able to straighten out her affairs and bring her to England. She needs our family, and what would it hurt for me to have a daughter?"

Fletcher cleared his throat. As a barrister, he had a need to discuss all legalities no matter how boring. "I still do not understand why Mr. Kensington decided to use an American company to settle his late son's affairs. My partners and I could have handled everything, and I would have sent a man to collect his granddaughter long before now. The girl needn't have suffered."

"Oh, I do not think she suffered in the way you are thinking." Gigi patted Fletcher's leg, a common way for her to calm his excitement. "She lost both her parents at one time. Each of you can sympathize with her, as you are still mourning your father."

Although they were out of the official mourning period by three months, it was still heart-wrenching to think about their father. His death had been sudden. As far as Baxter was aware, there hadn't been any indication of the late earl's illness. His father had collapsed during an evening with friends and never regained consciousness. By all accounts, it was a painless ending.

Baxter couldn't speak for the emotions welling up inside constricting his throat. He was thankful his mother yet lived, and he knew it would be a terrible burden upon a person to lose both parents at one time. If he had to endure a small amount of gossip around the neighborhood, he would do it to help alleviate the pain of Miss Kensington's loss. Gathering his wits, Baxter knew his mother needed his support. "I agree, Gigi. Please offer Miss Kensington and Mr. Kensington an invitation to dine at Primrose Hall before the week is out."

"I think I will add the Benton's to our supper party. Can you think of anyone else?"

Baxter shook his head. "You would have to invite all of Yorkshire to make the table even, Mother."

"True."

"You and Father should have realized this before you had seven sons." Baxter's admonition made his brothers chuckle. It had been a source of trouble having too many men and not enough couples at small parties. Inviting the Bentons meant Audrey and her elder brother Fredrick would attend, but that added another male to the table, and their younger daughter wasn't old enough for a supper party, and so it went with every family they dined with around Yorkshire.

"Better yet, Gigi and Father should have found a home near a family with seven daughters. We could have always had even meals if there was such a daring couple." Fletcher's need for practicality came out in these instances. At times he mused everyone to the point of boredom, but this was a valid solution to the issue.

With his brothers focused on finding a family of seven daughters, all of whom had entered society and could attend a supper party, Baxter found himself wondering about Miss Kensington and her situation. Her grandfather had been friends with Baxter's father, and Baxter considered him a good man, but there was the issue of the rebellious son who'd left English soil to seek adventure outside of his duty to family. The late Mr. Kensington had never been satisfied with running an estate. The itch of adventure had stolen him away from his father and his inheritance. Such adventurous people didn't sit well with Baxter.

Baxter's eyes drew to Phineas, and the discontent toward his brother's future settled again upon his shoulders. Phineas had finished his education at Cambridge and hadn't yet decided what he would do with his life. He spent hours studying books on archeology, sketching artifacts in a journal, and plotting his travels. Baxter worried his brother would do the same as Mr. Kensington's son had. Phineas would one day leave England and their family for an adventure to find treasures yet undiscovered.

As the head of their family, losing one of his siblings to the wider world frightened him. He would be a failure if they didn't all marry and raise families in England. They needed to stay close enough for house parties and summers at Primrose Hall. In that moment, he made a vow to keep his family connected. It might not be possible, not with Phineas so determined to run off to Egypt, but he would endeavor to do so.

He would do everything within his power to persuade Phineas to find other interests within England. Baxter thought about finding Phineas a wife, a good woman to keep his brother close. He vaguely thought of matching Phineas with Miss Kensington, since his mother seemed predisposed to like the woman, but matching an adventurous brother with an American wouldn't make sense. With his poor luck, she'd drag Phineas across the pond within the first days of their marriage and they'd never return.

Chapter Six

Smoke billowed from the hearth, causing Briar to rush out of the drawing room with her embroidery covering her mouth. Coughing as she escaped into the hall, she noticed Parker as he ran past her to tend to the situation. Expelling the smoke she'd inhaled from her lungs, and assuring herself the house wasn't on fire, Briar decided fresh air would be necessary to regain her composure.

Upon exiting the house, she chose not to stay within the confines of the yard. She had yet to see the beauty of the estate. Unconcerned about the endless puddles of mud, Briar decided it was the perfect day for an outing. Navigating past the first puddles, Briar realized the pathway was terribly boring if she focused on the ground. Around her was a world filled with beauty, and she was missing it. Pausing along the path, she stood silently and gazed over waves of snow rippling across the fields as tiny rays peeked through the looming clouds, causing the flakes to sparkle. The beauty of her grandfather's estate brought peace to her heart. She could learn to love this place, she only needed time to settle in.

Pressing forward on her outing, Briar didn't want to miss another moment of beauty. She didn't have a need to keep her skirts clean, and so she decided to take each puddle as it came. Mud and water would not stop her from the enchanting fields of sparkling snow and sheep. She hadn't noticed the animals in the distance at first glance. With their wool coats, it was easy to miss how they blended into the snow.

Rounding a corner, Briar's attention was on the sheep as she walked into something hard, causing her to bounce backward. Water splashed around her as she landed on her backside in the snow and mud. When Briar looked up, her heart halted in her chest at the man standing in front of her.

His dark green wool coat was a stark contrast to the snow clinging to the trees behind him. He removed his hat to reveal neatly combed dark brown hair. She noticed his cravat glowed with an incandescent white as it folded around his neck with starched perfection.

"What are you doing out on a day like this?" His rich accent sent a flurry of falling snow in her stomach.

Gathering her wits, Briar tried to speak but found herself frazzled and unhelpfully tongue-tied. She'd never seen such a tall and handsome man in all her life. To be fair, she'd met handsome well-mannered men in Boston, but they'd never made her heart pound in her ears.

"Are you injured? I live around the bend. I can help you to my home."

Her silence was dreadfully unhelpful. So, Briar accepted his outstretched hand and allowed him to pull her to her feet. As she placed her feet firmly on the ground, she vaguely acknowledged a sharp pain in her ankle. "Thank you for your assistance."

"You are the American?"

Was there a tinge of accusation in his statement? If there was, Briar was ready to meet the challenge, but she would be patient and decide if he meant to offend her before settling on any conclusions. "I am Briar Kensington."

"Miss Kensington, it is inappropriate for you to perform the introduction. Have you not a maid close by?" As he turned about looking for her companion to make an introduction, she decided his handsomeness waned a small amount. She couldn't deny her instant attraction to the man, but he was far too rigid with his mannerisms, and each word leaving his mouth left her wondering why he disapproved of her.

"I do not. I ventured out on my own today." She knew from the widening of his eyes and the backward step he took that there was an issue. It was possible she'd broken an important rule of British Society. Her nerves took hold, and she blundered her next statement. "It was such a lovely day. I did not want to stay indoors, and my maid refused to tromp around in the snow. She is a petite little thing, and the cold penetrates her skin much faster than it does mine."

"I see." Even though he'd said the words, Briar knew he certainly didn't mean them.

Did he truly understand her need to walk through the snowy fields and muddy paths? Did he understand the freedom she'd discovered in the brisk winter wind as it blew the top layer of snow across the fields? She was certain from his condemning, pointed gaze; he didn't care to know why she was alone. He didn't know anything about her, and yet this one meeting was forming every opinion he'd ever have. She also knew she wasn't innocent in her thinking. Her first impression of him wasn't anything to be repeated amongst Society.

As he continued speaking, Briar wondered if he ever smiled. His face looked far too serious for such a beautiful day. She decided his presence had been a blight upon her outing. "I will escort you back to Kensington Park."

Briar knew her dress was covered in mud from falling on the path. Also, her ankle was injured, but she wouldn't allow him to believe she was finished with her adventure. She'd been indoors far too much over the past weeks to go home so early. She also had the smoke billowing out of the drawing room hearth to consider. It couldn't possibly be remedied so quickly. She would need to stay out of doors for her health. Certainly, inhaling smoke was worse than the cold air. "No thank you, Mr.—" She didn't know his name since he'd so rudely forgotten to oblige her with an introduction.

"It is improper for us to continue speaking. Once I have you safely back at your grandfather's home, he can introduce us."

Briar raised one eyebrow in defiance. "I will not allow you to follow me home without your name. You are a stranger to me. How do I know your intentions are pure?"

"You should have considered such things before trespassing upon my property and stumbling into me like a bumbling American."

This man's way of saying *American* sounded like an insult and Briar would not take such insolence from anyone. "You are the one trespassing upon Kensington Park estate. This land belongs to my grandfather, and this is a fact I am willing to stake my life upon."

Irritation flashed in the deep blue eyes of the man whose erstwhile handsomeness had completely evaporated. She now thought him to be the ugliest man of her non-acquaintance. She could see he was making every effort to stay calm, and she inwardly applauded his self-control. "You are mistaken, Miss Kensington. The land you currently stand upon has been passed through six generations of my family and through the title of the Earl of Grafton. Mr. Kensington's land ended at the river you crossed to arrive at this point."

Briar had crossed a quaint stone bridge a while back. She felt a familiar heat creep across her cheeks as she realized she was wrong. Normally, she would apologize and make amends for her errors, but there was still the matter of his refusal to give her his name and how the way he'd called her a *bumbling American* had left her unsettled. To make matters worse, as she diverted her eyes to the ground, she noticed he'd walked along the same muddy pathway and had managed not to get a speck of mud upon his polished black Hessian boots.

Her spirits bolstered with all the defiance she could muster. Briar stared the man down. He must be one of Earl Grafton's sons. She was certain her grandfather had said their family name was Fernley. "Mr. Fernley, I apologize for my error, and I will ensure I do not cross onto the earl's land again."

The man was difficult to read as his eyes narrowed. "You will allow me to escort you back. You must be cold, and the disgraceful state of your clothing cannot go unattended."

This was one argument she wouldn't lose, even if her ankle was injured and she was ready for a warm bath and tea. "No. I am fully aware of the path I took to get to this point, and I will find my way home when I am ready."

"Do not be so disagreeable. If you will allow me to escort you home, I will explain your condition to your grandfather so there is not any question to your reputation."

"Is one's reputation so fragile, here in Yorkshire?"

"For a lady, yes."

"Then you should not want to be anywhere near me, sir, for I would not think it wise to let everyone know you are the reason my dress is covered in mud."

His lips curled with disgust as he took in her ruined clothing. "I most certainly am not responsible for your current state."

Elation surged through her, lending her a sense of pride as she considered his disgust at her muddy clothing. Instantly deciding Mr. Fernley needed a woman to oppose his piety, Briar dedicated herself to the task. Vexing this pious man would be a glorious addition to her outing. "You pushed me into a pool of mud and melted snow. How dare you suggest I did this to myself?"

Lowering his voice, Mr. Fernley defensively tilted his head. "What are you accusing me of? Do you seriously think a ploy like this will get me to offer for your hand?"

Briar's ankle shrieked in pain as she backed away from him. Marriage? How did they get to that? She only wanted him to apologize for ruining her outing. Her head spun and the world titled as the pain in her ankle increased. She wanted to turn and run away from the strict, unyielding man, but she couldn't with an injured ankle and her skirts heavy with mud.

"Miss Kensington, I have had women and their mothers more skilled than you in the art of matchmaking and ruin try to force my hand into a marriage. It comes with my position and title. I will not allow an uncultured foreigner to cause a stir over a clumsy moment on a cold—"

Briar lost all sense of propriety. He'd gone too far with his accusations. "How dare you accuse me of being uncultured? As for marriage, you are the last man in all the world I would ever want to offer for my hand."

"Miss Kensington, I am not so new to Society to think a woman such as yourself is not looking for an advantageous match. Admit the frailty of your attempt, and we can move past this very improper meeting."

"You are an odious, unfeeling, and unkind wretch." Briar had dealt with her share of suitors determined to collect her extensive dowry, but Mr. Fernley's unfounded assumptions left her infuriated. She'd never physically lashed out at anyone, especially a man, but this one deserved to be slapped. Unfortunately, her hand was closed due to the cold and Briar's dirty wet-gloved fist met Mr. Fernley's eye with more strength than she'd expected.

Realizing what she'd done, Briar backed away with her hand over her mouth from the irrational Mr. Fernley, who was rubbing the spot on his upper cheek where she'd hit him. As pain shot through her ankle, a high-pitched ringing sounded in her ears. Her ankle gave out, and Briar found herself again on the ground. And then she was in Mr. Fernley's arms as he carried her without her permission to a home much larger than Kensington Park.

Briar wouldn't allow this man to carry her away from her grandfather's estate without a fight. Even though she knew she was being impossible, she wouldn't give Mr. Fernley the satisfaction of playing the gentleman.

"Unhand me, you wretched man."

"Miss Kensington, I would suggest you thank me for my assistance before I drop you on your backside and leave you in the cold."

"You would not dare!" Although she didn't want him to play the hero, she also knew her ankle wouldn't hold her weight. It was far too injured.

"If you continue on in this manner, I will have no other choice."

"What do you mean by such a statement?" She would punish the man for his insensitive comments, if ever she had the opportunity.

"You are behaving like an absurd child. Exactly what I would expect from an American."

Briar gave a disapproving, unladylike harumph and turned her nose up as she looked away from him. She planned to never cross the bridge again. She would stay on Kensington Park's estate to avoid this rogue and his unfounded assumptions of her character. She may be an American, but it need not be an accusation and he need not concern himself over her welfare in the future.

Chapter Seven

" I admit, I lost my temper. The woman is so disagreeable." Baxter paced the parlor holding a poultice to his eye while waiting for Mr. Kensington and the physician to emerge from the upstairs chamber where he'd deposited Miss Kensington. He worried her ankle was more than injured—he feared a break. In any normal situation, he would have taken the liberty of assessing the damage before sending for a physician. But with her disagreeable attitude and his accusations of trapping him in a marriage, he had decided it was best to send for help.

He'd carried her directly into Primrose Hall and called for servants to see to her needs. When he'd ensured she wasn't in any danger of catching a chill, he sent two footmen out into the cold: one to Kensington Park and the other to the nearest physician. The biggest mistake he'd made since arriving at Primrose Hall with a maiden in his arms was relaying the entire ordeal to his family.

"Miss Kensington is a delightful young lady. You will discover this once you get to know her." Gigi found the entire situation amusing while his brothers snickered behind his back.

"Are you posting the banns?" Archibald asked, his somber tone interrupted with gales of laughter from their younger brothers. "You have the local vicar right here. All you need say is, Gilbert, my dear brother, announce my betrothal starting this Sunday."

Gilbert cleared his throat and straightened his waistcoat. "I wonder if it would be best to obtain a special license. You do seem in a rush, Baxter."

Baxter threw himself into a chair and glared at each of his brothers in turn. He'd done his fair share of teasing over the years but hated it when it came back to haunt him. "I do not find any of you to be amusing. Miss Kensington was injured, and I made a fool out of myself thinking she was expecting an offer of marriage. I do not know what came over me."

"None of us will deny that you have had your fair share of determined mothers chasing you during the season with their daughters in tow. But poor Miss Kensington did not deserve such treatment." Gilbert was right, and Baxter begrudgingly admitted he owed her an apology.

But he also needed his family to understand his position and the reason he had behaved so irrationally. Once they fully understood the situation as he saw it, they would not fault him for the ridiculous manner in which he'd behaved. "I was thrown off balance by the inappropriate way she barreled into me and then introduced herself with such imprudent manners. It was disconcerting. I would like to know where her maid was during this entire ordeal. Does Miss Kensington not understand the rules of propriety?"

"Baxter," Cornelius said, "you will one day realize heart and mind are better suited in these types of situations than adhering to staunch propriety."

Baxter watched as Gigi slowly lowered her sewing to look at Cornelius. Since joining the King's Army, Cornelius would make offhanded comments causing concern in their mother. This was one of those moments.

"I raised all of my sons to be proper gentleman, no matter the path they take in life."

"Oh Gigi, you misunderstand what I am saying." Cornelius shook his head and walked to the window. He'd become contemplative of late, and Baxter worried there was something terribly wrong with his brother. "Propriety is important, but is it also not necessary to consider the heart in these types of situations? Poor Miss Kensington will think we are ghastly, ill-mannered people all because the very proper and unyielding Earl Grafton met her along the road and caused her significant distress."

Baxter didn't consider himself unyielding. He thought it was a terribly off-putting way to describe his interlude with Miss Kensington. Also, none of them had been present for the entire debacle, and although the young lady would have an injured ankle, he was certain his eye would be bruised. Pressing the poultice firmly against his upper cheek, Baxter hoped it would soften the swelling. "I did not mean her any harm. In the future, I will take a moment to consider the situation I am in, especially if the young woman is skilled at fisticuffs."

"Before you start accusing the woman of secrecy and treachery?" Gilbert asked.

Baxter nodded. "Yes." He should have ended his comment there, but he unwisely continued to speak. "But in my defense, she is a traitorous American. The Commonwealth will never be the same since her people rose up and defied the laws of our land." With the encouragement of smiles from his brothers, Baxter continued. "Why, if I did not know Miss Kensington had been born long after the Colonist Uprising, I would stake my life on the claim that she was personally responsible for King George III being touched in the head."

When no one laughed, Baxter closed his eyes and took a deep breath to calm himself. Their silence was an indication that they were no longer alone. As he slowly turned toward the door leading out to the vestibule, he found his audience had grown to include the doctor,

Mr. Kensington, and Miss Kensington, who was in the arms of one of the footmen. Baxter instantly stood to acknowledge the arrival of a female.

Mr. Kensington's lips twitched as he held back a laugh. Miss Kensington looked ready to jump out of the footman's arms so she could punish Baxter for his insolence. The physician didn't hold back. He chuckled, clearly amused.

"Lord Grafton," Mr. Kensington said as he entered the room. "I assure you, my granddaughter had nothing to do with our King's current condition."

"Mr. Kensington, I did not hear you enter. I apologize for my outburst." Baxter refused to look at Miss Kensington for fear the seething hatred she must feel for him would make him shrivel to the size of a pebble.

"Although you have already met my granddaughter, I do feel it is necessary to give a proper introduction, but perhaps we should wait for a time when she has not driven you to such distraction."

The statement bothered Baxter, but only because it had a large amount of truth to it and far too much conjecture. Miss Kensington disturbed him in a way no other woman ever had, and he didn't enjoy the discomfort of not knowing how to think or feel when speaking with her. "I will see you out."

Mr. Kensington's smile broke free of his determination to keep a straight face. Baxter squirmed under the scrutiny of the man. The smile communicated much more than amusement. It assumed an attraction Baxter didn't feel. Thankfully, Mr. Kensington's tone was formal. "Thank you, my lord."

Baxter stayed by his chair with his eyes determinedly focused on anything except Miss Kensington as Mr. Kensington said farewell to each of Baxter's brothers and Gigi. When it was time, Baxter made his way out to Mr. Kensington's carriage. Stepping into a puddle, water splashed up his well-polished boots, forcing him to pay attention to his surroundings. He'd never been so distracted in all his life.

He stood rigidly next to the carriage, ensuring Miss Kensington was covered in a blanket and a brick was placed below her seat before he closed the door upon her offended, tight-lipped countenance. As the carriage left Primrose Hall, Baxter closed his eyes in an attempt to refocus his thoughts. He didn't need an American, no matter how pretty she was, to leave him unsettled.

Chapter Eight

Briar's ankle still hurt days after the incident, but the wrap helped enable her to limp around the house. Sitting with her feet propped up on the sofa, Briar was surprised when Lady Grafton and her son entered the parlor. Although it was her designated visiting hours, she hadn't expected anyone. She chose not to stand for the insufferable man's arrival. Instead, she stayed firmly planted on the cushions of her cozy sofa. She didn't mean any disrespect to Lady Grafton, so she kept her snarl for the man entering with his mother.

"Lord Grafton, my granddaughter, Miss Kensington." Her grandfather was always proper in everything he said and did. Therefore, she was wholly unsurprised with the formal introduction. The introduction she knew the odious man needed so he could socialize.

"Lord Grafton?" Briar said heat rising in her cheeks. "You said your name was Fernley."

"No, Miss Kensington, I told you it was inappropriate for us to perform an introduction without a common acquaintance."

Briar wasn't as uncivilized as Lord Grafton believed, so she nodded in acknowledgment and bit back her retort. She wanted to argue with him and tell him he had misrepresented himself when they'd first met, but she stopped as she realized he was telling the truth. He'd never introduced himself, which was one of the reasons she'd been so put out with him.

"Miss Kensington, I owe you an apology." Lord Grafton's lips turned up in a pained expression she was certain he meant as a smile, but it left her wondering if he was ill. Was an apology so difficult for the loathsome earl to make? "I should never have accused you of seeking to entrap me in a marriage. I also should not have implicated you as a reason for King George's infirmities."

The proper reaction to an apology would be to accept it and forgive the person, so Briar pushed the pain of his comments aside and acknowledged Lord Grafton's words. "I promise never to expect an offer of marriage from you. As for King George III, I can make no promises."

A strained silence filled the room, and Briar wondered if her words about the king had been taken seriously. She'd meant it in jest and had hoped for some lighthearted banter to follow. However, Lord Grafton looked shocked, and the Dowager Countess exchanged a strained glance with Briar's grandfather. Briar wondered if she was truly too American, as Lord Grafton had accused her of being. Had she committed a social faux pas without realizing it?

She waited, worried another word out of her mouth would bring further shame to her grandfather. She loved the man and did not wish any harm upon him or his home. He'd graciously brought her to England when there were no other options in Boston. Repaying such kindness with insult would be terribly wrong.

"I will alert the Royal Guard of the tyrannical colonist you brought to our shores, Mr. Kensington." Lord Grafton's eyes lit up with mischief.

This was the type of banter she'd hoped for, yet the delay had marred the moment. Instead of a quick-witted reply, Briar blushed and hung her head in shame. She stayed silent as the conversation turned to the weather, neighbors she didn't know, and the presence of all seven Fernley sons at Primrose Hall. She was wishing her ankle had been further injured, forcing her to stay in her bedchamber away from such dull conversation, when her grandfather pulled her attention back to the group.

"I will not further delay my purpose in asking you here today."

This was surprising, and Briar found her face reddening again with the realization that Lord Grafton hadn't come out of a sense of duty with an apology. He'd come at the behest of her grandfather.

Her grandfather adjusted in his seat, hesitating to find the right words. "I received a letter from my late son's solicitor of a situation in France. I will need to attend to matters in person."

Briar's curiosity piqued. Her father had spent every other year in France. The travel between the states and the continent had made his duty to the family business burdensome. "My father was in France often, for business. I would love to visit his home there and meet people who knew him."

"I am afraid I cannot take you with me."

Briar thought personal matters constituted inappropriate conversation to have in front of guests, but she wasn't going to allow her grandfather to push her aside. She'd asked her father many times to take her to France, but he'd never agreed. Now that he was gone, she desired to go even more.

"I think it would be the perfect way to honor my father's life. Please, grandfather, I have not yet had time to make friends, and you promised not to leave until I had someone I could prevail upon for help." Reminding him of his promise had been a tactic to help him make the decision to take her along, but he didn't budge.

"You have made friends, or at least acquaintances, at Primrose Hall. Lord Grafton has agreed to be your protector while I am away."

Briar blinked a few times, speechless with the plans her grandfather had made on her behalf. He hadn't asked for her opinion, and it seemed everyone in the room expected her to comply without question. Staying at the home of a stranger would be far more enjoyable than spending another moment in the company of the illustrious and ill-mannered Lord Grafton.

"I would prefer to live on the streets of Boston than to stay under the protection of Lord Grafton."

"Briar, do not be unreasonable. Lady Grafton will be there to keep everything proper between you and the earl."

Heat rushed up her neck, and her mouth fell open at the simple statement. Perhaps other women would need a chaperone to keep them from falling apart in an earl's presence, but Briar didn't need such a person.

"I am aware of your dislike for me," Lord Grafton said as he casually lounged in his chair. The quizzical confusion he'd shown earlier was completely removed from his face. He sat in a state of confidence, and she despised him for it. Even the fading purple and yellow of his bruised eye didn't give her satisfaction. She wanted nothing to do with the repulsive earl. "I will not allow our previous encounter to mar your visit to Primrose Hall. With the assistance of my mother and younger brothers, I believe you will have an enjoyable stay."

Briar turned away from the boastful earl. His reaction told her he was enjoying her discomfort. The hateful, odious man made her glare at her grandfather hoping to bring him to submission. She hadn't lost the argument, not yet. "Why can I not stay at Kensington Park? Lord Grafton and his accommodating brothers can check on me each day, and then I will not cause undue stress upon the household at Primrose Hall."

"I do not want to spend my entire trip worrying over your welfare. Lord Grafton has agreed to protect you while I am traveling, and you will accept his gracious offer."

Briar was not one to hold her tongue, especially when she was certain she was the only one with a bit of common sense. "Grandfather, I spent the last year caring for myself while you made arrangements to bring me to England, and although you paid Mr. and Mrs. Holstead to accompany me across the ocean, I spent much of my time by myself. I am a capable woman who does not need a governess."

Lord Grafton scoffed in disgust. "I am not a governess, nor am I a nurse maid. You are welcome to stay at my home if your pride will allow it."

Briar had nothing kind to say to the earl, so she kept her eyes locked on her grandfather. "You will not leave me at the mercy of this unfeeling man."

Her grandfather chuckled. Much to her surprise, he was enjoying the argument between her and Lord Grafton. "I am afraid it cannot be helped. I must attend to this situation on my own. Lord Grafton is not as unworthy as you currently claim. You have yet to know of his goodness."

"What could be so important to take you away right after my arrival? You did not travel to the states to find me. What is more important than my safety?" She knew her words would be used against her to argue for the arrangements with Lord Grafton, but she'd already lost that battle. Now she needed to know why her grandfather planned to leave.

"It is not necessary for you to concern yourself over matters of your father's finances. I will discover if the claim is credible and decide how to handle the situation. Knowing you are safe will ease this parting."

"But I only just arrived in England."

Her grandfather leaned forward and took hold of her hands. "I will not be away long."

Briar wondered if it was possible for him to make such a promise without full knowledge of the financial situation in France. Any number of problems could arise to separate them, but she decided to accept her grandfather's statement and begrudgingly accept her fate. She would have to stay with Lord Grafton's family for the rest of winter. If she had any luck, she would stay clear of the detestable man and spend her time alone.

Chapter Nine

Although she knew further argument would get her nowhere, Briar gave her grandfather one last pleading gaze as the carriage turned up the drive to Primrose Hall. She put an extra emphasis into her pout, hoping the pathetic nature of her features would break him of his decision to leave her behind. "I had hoped you would decide to take me with you."

"It is not possible, Briar. Please do not make this parting any more difficult than it already is."

Showing her displeasure at his insistence, Briar refused to look at her grandfather. She sat with her arms folded and her head turned toward the window. Her eyes glazed over, and all she saw was a blanket of snow with intruding trees as they passed by. "What if Lord Grafton and I spend the entire time arguing? It will make me a very unwanted guest."

"You will need to be agreeable. Men do not care for vexing females."

Briar quickly turned toward her grandfather and gave him a glare of distrust. She worried he had misplaced hope in a match with the earl. "Why should I care for his good opinion?"

EARL GRAFTON AND THE TRAITOR

"Do not dismiss the earl too soon, my dear. I believe he finds you worth his notice."

"Yet, I find him beneath mine."

She understood her grandfather's sigh to mean he didn't find her pouting amenable to the situation. "If you will remember, I suggested one of the Fernley men would make a good match for you. I hope you will use your time at Primrose Hall to make connections and form an attachment."

Shocked by her grandfather's statement, Briar felt heat rising into her cheeks. Suddenly, his motives for leaving her in England while he traveled to France were clear. Had he concocted a reason to leave the country? Was this all a ruse to marry her off to one of the earl's brothers? "Grandfather, I cannot stay at Primrose Hall knowing you expect me to make a match. It is inappropriate."

"Briar, I am an old man, and one day I will leave this world and you will be left without me. I want to know you are well cared for and loved. While I am away, I urge you to do all you can to find a husband. I have asked Lady Grafton to make introductions for you, and she is aware of my desire for your future."

She wanted to argue, but how could she with his concern so evident? She couldn't deny the trouble she'd be in if he were to die. It would be much like she'd experienced upon the death of her parents. For over a year she'd been passed between friends and relatives, none of whom wanted to care for her. If she lost her grandfather, she would have nowhere to go. Logically, marriage was the answer. But her heart refused to believe it was necessary to rush into a marriage. "You could yet live many more years. Please, let us not concern ourselves over the future but focus on each moment we have together."

"No, Briar." Her grandfather's strict admonishment left her momentarily speechless. She listened but wanted to fight each word and deny the possibility of losing another person in her life. "My duty is to make certain you are cared for. I have given Lord Grafton

51

permission and access to pay out your dowry upon your marriage. Before I return to England, I expect to receive word of an engagement."

Briar chose not to speak to her grandfather for the rest of the short journey to the front of Primrose Hall. She wasn't surprised to find Lord Grafton and his family awaiting her arrival. Nor was she surprised to be received by the housekeeper and butler. The same had occurred upon her arrival at her grandfather's home weeks before. Trying to keep her emotions under control, Briar embraced her grandfather and silently watched his carriage as it swiftly left her standing with people who were merely acquaintances.

It felt very much like when her parents had died. The grief never wore off for her, but those who'd been entrusted with her well-being wanted their lives to go back to normal, and a permanent visitor was unwelcome. She'd despised every day with those insincere people wishing her parents would not have died, and when she'd received the letter from her grandfather, a new hope had emerged, leaving her with the desire for a life with real family. But the backside of the carriage left her where she'd begun. Lord Grafton had graciously offered to let her stay in his home. He would be her protector. But she was also very aware of the fact that he didn't care for her, and therefore, it was easy to assume it wouldn't be long before she wore out her welcome.

SETTLING INTO THE NEW ROOM AT PRIMROSE HALL HAD been seamless, with the housekeeper showing her to her bedchamber and her maid taking charge of her clothing. Briar stood by the window appreciating the view. It had snowed during the night, leaving the earth pristine with glistening flakes resting upon the window ledge. Icicles hung from tree branches like leaves, and the newness of the powdery snow made her thankful she was indoors with a fire in the hearth. Off in the distance, a stone tower stood majestically surrounded by puffy snow resembling clouds, distracting her from the worries pushing upon her shoulders. She wanted to know what the building was and how it had fallen to ruin.

As she studied the ruins out her window, she wanted to find her way across the fields and discover the mystery of what lay between the ancient walls. Since arriving in Yorkshire, she'd spent far too much time alone wishing for something to do. Now with the ruins on her mind, she wanted to either discover the truth or make up stories for the people who'd once lived in the magical place.

With her mind fully occupied, Briar jumped and let out a startled scream as a hand touched her. Heart pounding in her chest at the interruption, she tried to recover quickly while placing a hand over her chest.

"Miss Kensington, I did not mean to startle you." Lady Grafton stood next to Briar, her hand on Briar's elbow. "What has you so preoccupied? I called your name twice."

"I was enjoying the view."

Lady Grafton smiled and picked out the exact edifice in Briar's thoughts. "It was a grand home at one time."

"What happened? Why did it fall into disrepair?"

"There was a fire. The first Earl of Grafton was an eccentric man, and he set the house a flame. At the time, Primrose Hall was a hunting lodge, but upon the death of the first earl, his son made this home what it is today. It took nearly his entire life to finish the work on the house, but it is as grand as the first home once was."

Briar experienced a sudden and severe sense of sadness over the loss of the home. "Do you know why he set the fire?"

"Family lore states it was due to the death of his wife and newborn child. The vicar at the time recorded the two deaths three days before the earl died. Journals from the second earl and his siblings give us a deeper look into the situation. The earl lost his mind upon the death of his wife and tenth child."

"How tragic!" Briar placed a hand over her mouth at the emotions bubbling up over the terrible circumstances that had led to the majestic ruins upon the hill. She could relate to the first earl. She well knew the pain of losing loved ones. Such loss could destroy all sensibility, and she was convinced he'd acted out of grief.

"It is a part of our ancestry that has never been forgotten."

"Is that why the walls and tower are still standing?"

"Yes. No one has the heart to remove the final memory of such sadness."

"It is a magnificent view. I am thankful for this room and for your hospitality." Briar hoped to make herself as invisible as possible. If she wasn't a burden, they might not regret accepting her into their home. Although she didn't care to know Lord Grafton, she had to admit Primrose Hall was magnificent. She could almost forgive his impertinence with such beauty to distract her, but then she remembered his accusation of her being a traitorous American, and she decided her forgiveness was not yet earned.

"We are happy to have you here, and I will not hear of you spending all your time in this bedchamber. You are welcome at Primrose Hall. Now, you should take time to rest as I am certain after supper activities with my sons will make you weary. They are a lively group."

The sincerity in Lady Grafton's eyes left Briar hopeful that this visit would be much different than what she'd been through with her cousins. She would love to feel a part of such a large family, and even though her grandfather wanted her to make a match with one of the boys, Briar hoped most of all she would find friends. Making a careful decision, Briar decided she would spend the evening testing out her presence in their home. If they were kind and accepting, she would do as Lady Grafton asked and not stay alone in her chambers. "I cannot wait to meet each one."

As Lady Grafton took her leave, Briar turned back to the ruins. The story she'd started imagining was far less romantic than what had actually happened. She'd made up a narrative that included invasion and war, but the loss of loved ones was something she could relate to, and tears formed in the corners of her eyes. She didn't bother to wipe them away, for she knew it would be futile. Wrapping her arms tightly around her middle, Briar lost track of time as a fog went over her mind, blocking out the ruins with memories of her parents, the ache of loss, and the feeling that nothing would be right again. Losing loved ones would never be easy, nor should it be.

WHEN BRIAR ENTERED THE DRAWING ROOM BEFORE supper, she was still emotional over having been dropped off at Primrose Hall and the memories of her parents. Of course, she knew the feelings of abandonment and loss stemmed from her parents' death. The heartache was close to the surface, but no matter how much she'd wanted to curl up under her bedcovers and forget about supper, she couldn't. It would be improper and ungrateful for her to stay in her chambers for the night.

With a formal introduction to everyone in the room, she smiled at the thought that each of the men's names would be easily remembered as they were all Mr. Fernley. The exception was Lord Grafton, and she wouldn't have a difficult time remembering his obnoxious name.

As the butler announced dinner, Briar was surprised to find Lord Grafton offering his arm to her. Her grandfather had done the same since she'd arrived, but she hadn't expected or even wanted Lord Grafton to escort her into supper. Nervously, she accepted his arm to avoid a scene, and she walked with as much grace as she could muster. To her disappointment, she was seated to the right of Lord Grafton, who sat at the head of the table.

As the first round was presented, Briar's attention was pulled to the end of the table where Mr. Phineas Fernley sat. He'd called out to her, and the conversation surprisingly put her at ease.

"Miss Kensington, do tell us about Boston. I have always wanted to speak with an American."

Her mood quickly changed from melancholy to pleasure. This was a topic she loved and could converse on with ease. "I would be honored. Do you have plans to travel?"

Phineas's excitement pushed all of Briar's previous worries about not fitting in and being a burden to the back of her mind. She instantly felt a kinship with this man. "I do wish to visit the former colonies one day, but first I would like to go to Egypt and crawl around in the pyramids and ancient tombs."

This was not what she expected to hear. She knew Society frowned upon men who didn't conform to their expectations. She expected each of the men sitting at the table would be searching for a woman who was considered a diamond of the first water with a dowry to support them for the rest of their lives.

"Oh?"

"Yes. I have spent the last ten years studying and making notes on the pyramids, pharaohs, Cleopatra, and the Valley of the Kings. I hope to spend time digging for artifacts that can give us deeper insight into the rich history of the ancient world."

Briar found this fascinating and would have asked questions if she knew anything relevant about Egypt. However, she didn't know what to ask and wouldn't have had a chance as Lord Grafton ruined the pleasant discussion with his uncouth behavior.

"You would prefer to spend your life in the desert than with your family?" Lord Grafton's dismay made Briar curious. It was obvious Grafton wasn't angry over his brother's desire to leave England, but it distressed him greatly. He had a strained look about him.

"Baxter, you know I have no desire to settle down and marry. I want to be free to live my life as I choose. And if that means I'll spend it covered in dirt while I dig for artifacts in the Egyptian desert, then you should support me in my choice."

Briar made a mental note to inform her grandfather that Phineas was not a possible match. He'd clearly stated he didn't intend to marry, and therefore, she would form a friendship with the man. She was thankful to have taken two of the eligible bachelors in the home off the list of possible suitors: Phineas and Lord Grafton. She now had five more men to exclude.

"What of Gigi and her health? Do you not care about her?" Lord Grafton argued.

Phineas bowed his head, his shoulders slumped, as he refused to look at anyone in his family. "Gigi understands my desire for adventure, and Father did as well. He encouraged me to find my place in the world."

"I am the head of this family now, and I will not allow you to leave England."

"You cannot stop me from pursuing my dreams. Your jurisdiction is for the estate. You cannot control my life."

Briar looked between the earl and Phineas, worried about her place in the argument. She hadn't caused it, but her presence had invoked the conversation. Should she apologize? Should she keep silent? At her cousin's home, she'd accidently caused an argument that had lasted for days. Even after she had apologized, her presence was never truly wanted again. She'd taken meals in her chambers for the rest of her time at that home. She glanced at Lady Grafton to offer an apology, but the woman's kind smile conveyed a message of peace. If she understood the woman's expression, there was no need for the anxious tightening within Briar's chest.

Lady Grafton stood, which caused her sons to scramble to their feet. When they were silent, she retook her seat and waited for her sons to resume their positions. "Now that I have your attention," she said, looking at Lord Grafton first and then Phineas, "need I remind you we have a guest in our home?"

"No, Gigi, I apologize for my behavior." Lord Grafton's apology left Briar stunned. She'd misjudged the earl, at least partially. His humble respect for Lady Grafton trumped his title and ownership of the estate.

"I am not the only one who deserves your apology."

Much to Briar's surprise, Lord Grafton turned to her. "Miss Kensington, will you please accept my heartfelt repentance for causing discord within my family? You did not deserve a display of our reckless manners."

Speechless over the apology, Briar nodded. She had very little time to formulate a response or even consider one before Phineas was apologizing to her as well. As dinner progressed, Briar noticed it didn't take long for everyone to start speaking again. The atmosphere changed back to a level of comfort, and it seemed the argument was forgotten.

The anxious concern of moments before lessened, and the heaviness of being a burden lifted. Briar engaged in a conversation with Lady Grafton about lace and muslin. Somehow, Briar knew she was fully welcome in their home, and she hadn't had such a pleasant feeling since she'd last sat with her parents.

Chapter Ten

Baxter pulled at his cravat as he entered the dining room. The tight knot pressing against his neck loosened. When he found Miss Kensington breakfasting alone, he thought about leaving. Supper the evening before had been embarrassing. He'd made an absolute fool out of himself when arguing with Phineas. He would need to speak with his brother, but accosting him in the middle of supper in front of a guest was not appropriate.

The proper choice would have been to allow Miss Kensington to delight them with tales of Boston. He was not as unbending as everyone thought. He would like to know about the former colonies and the beauty of that land. He didn't have any desire to travel there, but that didn't mean he had little care for stories about the place.

As her head came up, he knew his escape should have happened before she had noticed his presence. It would be terribly rude for him to back out, so he decided to go about his day as usual. He could handle polite conversation without help and without making a ninny of himself.

"Good morning, Miss Kensington." Baxter bowed his head in her direction and then set about preparing a plate while chiding himself for being so formal. He was nervous, and it was causing his manners to be stiff. He knew Miss Kensington despised the stiff earl.

Her wide eyes and worried expression told him he was right; he'd spoiled the morning by being so formal. "Lord Grafton, I did not expect anyone to be up so early. If you would prefer, I shall take my meal in my chambers."

Baxter closed his eyes and took a deep breath to calm himself. His heart was racing, and his hands had gone cold with sweat. He hadn't meant anything rude with his greeting. He'd hoped to make her feel welcome and somehow find a way to form a friendship. "Not at all. You are welcome to any of the public rooms in the house."

"Thank you, my lord." Her clipped response left him in no doubt of his mistake. "It is only that I have noticed you prefer to be anywhere but in the same room as me, and I did not want to cause you distress."

"On the contrary, Miss Kensington, I have no such feelings when you are nearby." It wasn't true. The flutter in his chest was enough to mock his claim of self-control. As he took hold of a serving spoon to dish eggs onto his plate, his hand jerked, and eggs dumped onto the sideboard. Taking a moment to compose himself, he steadied his hand and successfully dished a sufficient amount of food onto his plate.

"I am well aware of the strain a guest can have on a home. My cousins were not happy to have me when I needed a place to stay, and I found it better to stay in my chambers on most occasions. I can do so here if it will make the situation more bearable for you."

The pretty pink morning dress she wore accented the blush in her cheeks so perfectly, he found himself at a loss for words. He didn't want her to stay in her chambers, and he found the confession of how she'd been treated to be abhorrent.

"My lord, are you unwell?" Miss Kensington leaned toward him. Her eyes narrowed in concern. "Perhaps you should spend your day resting."

Finding his voice, Baxter shook his head. "I am only preoccupied." It was the truth. Finding her alone in the dining room had left him completely boorish with a lack of anything kind and good to say. He couldn't take the pain she'd suffered away, but he could make her feel welcome at Primrose Hall. "Miss Kensington, you do not need to worry about your presence in my home. You are welcome here, and I am happy to have you as my guest."

She examined him to see if there was truth in his words. He tried to smile but found his lips wouldn't curve up in the proper way and he was stuck with his serious earl persona. "Your statement is not accurate, but I thank you for making an effort."

Baxter unceremoniously dropped his plate on the table and glared at Miss Kensington. She was quite possibly the most frustrating woman all and sundry. Certain it was her goal in life to inflict the depths of insanity upon him, he clenched his jaw and kept his mouth shut. Taking his seat, Baxter pushed his plate to the side and picked up the daily newspaper. He needed to gather his thoughts. As he found an article to interest him, he finally decided upon a response. "Miss Kensington, in Boston people may treat each other with open rudeness, but the British are above such diatribe." It was an unfortunate response, and he knew it was the wrong one when her pretty blush turned a deeper shade of red and extended into her ears.

"No, my dear Lord Grafton, a more accurate statement would be to say the British are politely rude while wishing the person had never entered their grand estate."

Her statement was correct. He knew the women in Society could be intolerant, and he wondered if Briar had experienced such treatment since she'd arrived. She hadn't been in England long. "Has someone in our neighborhood treated you with polite rudeness?"

Miss Kensington stood, so Baxter followed suit. "Only you, my lord."

He watched as she walked away, questioning her statement. In all honesty, he had treated her with unkindness, but he was trying to be nice. As he retook his seat, he decided to make a greater effort at pleasing his guest. But most importantly, he would have to ignore her uncultured rudeness.

BAXTER CONTRIVED A PLAN BEFORE HE STEPPED THROUGH the large mahogany double doors to the drawing room. He had to resolve the situation with Phineas and convince his brother to stay in England. There were opportunities for archeologists in London. One well-placed referral could find him a teaching situation at Cambridge or Oxford. There were archeological sites within their country, and Baxter could arrange for Phineas to take part in local discoveries. His brother didn't need to travel to Egypt to take a role in uncovering artifacts and discovering history.

Upon entering, his eyes fell upon Miss Kensington as she laughed at something Oliver was saying. Oliver had the ability to charm women with his quick wit and charismatic personality. It was a talent Baxter lacked. He was far too serious for such interactions.

Amongst Oliver's finer qualities, he was a talented musician. As Miss Kensington slowly removed each glove, pressing them into Oliver's outstretched hand, Baxter waited to hear her play the piano. As she pressed her delicate fingers against the ivory keys, he stood transfixed in the moment. Miss Kensington was as accomplished as any other female of his acquaintance. He tried to acknowledge the fact without giving it much thought or preference in his mind. There were many ladies amongst the *ton* who played well; he need not care about this one.

Turning away from the pair, Baxter found Phineas and motioned with his head for his brother to follow him. As they walked down the hall to the den, Baxter checked his emotions to ensure he was calm.

He didn't want a repeat of the previous night's argument, and he didn't want to put Phineas in a defensive mood before the conversation started.

Upon entering the den, Baxter pointed to the overstuffed armchairs by the window. The conversation would be less official if he wasn't sitting behind the large mahogany desk. He'd also asked Ames to send up tea and fairy cakes, which were thankfully waiting for them on the small table between the chairs. If anyone were to stumble upon the conversation, it would look like two brothers enjoying afternoon tea.

Baxter motioned for the maid to pour, and then excused her from the room. "Phineas, I am truly sorry for accosting you at supper last night. I know you have dreamt of visiting Egypt for many years."

"Baxter, if this is an attempt at convincing me to stay in England, it will not work." Phineas had yet to take a seat. Instead, he stood near the window, his arms folded and his mouth tight with suspicion.

He couldn't be dishonest with his brother, and so he admitted his purpose to the tea and cakes. "I had hoped to soften your heart with the treats. But since you are determined to leave England, will you share your reasons with me? Help me understand what is happening in your head?"

"I have always wanted to travel. You know this."

Baxter let out a sigh of relief as Phineas let down his guard and sat. He needed to keep his temper in check and not cause an argument if this was to go well. Since his father's death, this was one of the hardest parts of his duty. His father had taken care of their family with what looked to be ease. Baxter's desire to keep Phineas in England had caused a bout of turmoil during supper, something his father never would have allowed to happen. He had much to learn if he was to emulate the man.

"Yes, but you never spoke about spending the rest of your life in Egypt before now. I thought you simply wanted to visit other coun-

ANGELA JOHNSON

tries and then settle here with a wife and children. What has changed?"

Phineas looked away, which told Baxter this was going to be a difficult conversation. He knew exactly what had changed, and he had no way of putting everything right. Their lives had turned upside down the day their father died.

"Primrose Hall is no longer home for me."

"Do not be ridiculous. You are welcome here, and if you prefer this as your permanent residence, I will make the arrangements."

Phineas chuckled while wiping at unwanted tears and shook his head. "I thank you for saying as much. But I need to find my place in the world, now that it no longer includes our father."

Baxter knew he had lost this argument before the conversation began. He'd been puffed up and foolish to believe it was a simple case of unrest. Just as he was trying to figure out his role as earl and magistrate, each of his brothers had to discover who they were as gentlemen. It was the path they were on, and Baxter was more than helpless because he couldn't fix anything for them. "What can I do to help?"

"Support my decisions, even when you disagree with me. Father knew of my desires to travel. He allowed me to study archeology knowing it would take me away from England, and he understood. I need you to give me that same trust and support."

"Have you discussed this with Gilbert? How will you survive without your twin to get you out of scrapes?"

Phineas smiled at the jest, and the tension lifted from their conversation. "Gil might not like the idea of being parted, but he understands. I asked him to leave this all behind and travel with me, but he prefers the boring life of a vicar."

Baxter closed his eyes and took a few calming breaths. He was thankful Gilbert was level-headed and ready to settle into the role of religious leader. One more brother leaving England would be the end of Baxter. He was already losing two, with Cornelius and his military duties and Phineas leaving for adventure. If one more decided to leave, Baxter would pass the title onto Archie and make certain his resting place was next to his father and sisters. It pained him to admit defeat, but he had to do it. And he had to be sincere. "You will always have a home here. When will you leave?"

"In the spring."

Baxter let out a distressed sigh. Every word out of Phineas's mouth left him anxious. "So soon?"

"Each day I delay is another day outside of my dreams. One day, I hope you understand and stop deferring your dreams with the excuse of your title."

Although he nodded his head, Baxter didn't understand. He didn't have the soul of a traveler. He loved England, the estate, and his ancestry. He was proud to be the one to carry on the title, and when he was ready, he would find a wife to give him heirs. "All I have ever wanted is to make Mother and Father proud of me. I will do that by fulfilling the duty that has fallen on my shoulders."

"I feel sorry for you, Baxter."

"Why?"

"Because you have never allowed yourself to dream."

Baxter took a sip of his tea. If he didn't understand his brother, he would have been offended by the statement. But he knew Phineas too well to take it as an insult. "Duty must come first, brother."

"I am thankful I was not born the heir. I would not be able to stay in one place for the rest of my life."

"Then you will have to write letters and regale me with tales of your grand adventures so I may be entertained in what you would consider my boredom."

"I promise to do so."

Baxter knew there was one more way he could show his support for his brother, and so he put aside his fears of losing another person in his life and picked up one of the jam-filled fairy cakes. Before taking a bite, he started asking questions. "Where do you plan to go first?"

Having a conversation with his brother about travels, archeology, and distant lands was easier than Baxter had originally thought it would be. He admired Phineas for the courage it would take to leave on an adventure. But very close to the surface was the hope that Phineas would one day find his way back to England and their family.

Chapter Eleven

"What are your plans for the day, Miss Kensington?" Lady Grafton set her embroidery to the side and looked at Briar with a motherly smile. Three days at Primrose Hall and Briar truly felt the warmth of home. She no longer feared being a burden upon Lord Grafton and his household. They'd all been so very welcoming; she truly felt a part of the family.

Since arriving, she'd wanted to snoop into every corner of the large house and discover its secrets. She'd never been in such a grand home. "I thought it might be interesting to look around the house, if you do not have any objections."

"None whatsoever. I think a guided tour would be best. There is so much history within the walls of Primrose Hall, and you will never know any of it if you walk the halls on your own."

Briar instantly shook her head. "I do not want to be a burden, Lady Grafton."

"Hush! If you do not stop with such silly comments, I will be forced to bore you with hours of embroidery." Lady Grafton laughed and then called out to her son. "Baxter, you do not seem to have anything pressing at the moment. Will you please show Miss Kensington the house?"

Lord Grafton's eyes were unreadable as he looked at his mother. "Gigi, I am certain one of my brothers would do a better job of it."

"They are previously occupied."

Briar wanted to argue with Lady Grafton and would even torture herself with embroidery if only to stay out of Lord Grafton's way. She was ready to search out one of the other men if a guide was needed. She'd managed to have purposeful conversations with Phineas and Oliver. She'd also managed to eliminate Oliver as a possible suitor. They had much in common and she would forever consider him the dearest of friends, but he was not a match for love.

Following a moment of awkward silence, Lord Grafton stepped forward and bowed his head in a very proper manner. Briar wondered if he ever let go of the rigid earl persona. "Miss Kensington, I would be delighted to guide you through the house."

Briar wondered what the word *delighted* meant to Lord Grafton, because he didn't show any signs of pleasure at the task. His stiff movements made her regret mentioning a tour.

"The home was originally called Primrose Lodge. The first Earl of Grafton used it to host large hunting parties. The original dwelling had seventeen bedrooms and consisted of five general living areas..."

Briar felt like she was on a tour being herded through beautiful rooms that could be interesting, if she wasn't with a guide who'd practiced the art of boredom. If she were going to enjoy the house, she would have to look around on her own when Lord Grafton was not relaying every historical detail of the walls and ceiling plaster.

She allowed him to leave her behind in the long hallways as she admired vases, paintings, and statues along the way. As she spied a yellow vase, she bent over to see the intricate carvings upon the lip and base. A faint smell of eucalyptus wafted close by as Briar realized Lord Grafton's voice wasn't trailing back to her. With the trepidation of a child caught in disobedient behavior, Briar slowly turned her head to find his piercing blue eyes focused upon her. She would never tell him, but his eyes reminded her of the beauty of the ocean.

"Is there a reason you have stopped?" Lord Grafton asked. His hands were firmly locked on his hips like he expected an answer for her dawdling.

"I wanted to look at the engraving on this vase."

Lord Grafton narrowed his gaze and then lifted the delicate yellow vase to his eye level. "It is simply a pattern of swirls. Now, I was ready to show you the family gallery."

"Yes, my lord." As they entered a long gallery filled with paintings, Briar ignored Lord Grafton's rhetoric on the art of choosing the perfect wall hangings and walked directly to the first painting on the wall. The man's eyes and sad countenance drew her soul into the artwork. Briar interrupted Lord Grafton's explanation on the purpose of the gold brocade. She needed to know who the man was in the painting. "Who is this?"

Crossing the empty space between them, Lord Grafton stood close enough for Briar to enjoy the scent of eucalyptus, but far enough away for propriety. "The first Earl of Grafton."

"Was it here before the fire?" She knew family art galleries were usually found within the walls of the family home, not a hunting lodge.

"No. It was removed from the original home."

Briar turned to Lord Grafton. "Then everything was not lost in the fire?"

"The eldest son was able to gather a few items before the house was destroyed." Grafton pointed to another portrait, which looked like a younger version of the first earl.

In between the two portraits was the first countess, the woman who had held the heart of the earl and whose death had been the reason for the devastating loss of the original home. Even if it was the artist who made her look pleasant, Briar immediately felt a kinship to her cheerful countenance. "I wonder why a woman with so much life

69

in her would marry a man who looked so mournful. He did not even smile for his likeness."

She didn't care for an answer, but Lord Grafton provided one that left her rooted to the spot. She didn't want to move without reconciling his words to match the romantic hopes of her heart. "You will find, Miss Kensington, that marriages in England are about wealth and titles. Love has often been far from the minds of those entering into the institution."

"Then why would the earl have been so distraught over his wife and child dying, if he was not in love?"

"He had nine other children. Can you imagine raising that many children and finding husbands for all the daughters without a wife to help? The poor fool knew he was a lost cause. He didn't want the responsibility, and so he passed it to his son."

Briar turned to Lord Grafton, her eyes narrowed in astonishment. "What a horribly wicked thing to say about the man. You consider his sorrow to be selfish?"

"Yes, I do. Why, what do you imagine when you look at the man?"

"I choose to believe he loved his wife and could not find a way to live without her."

"You have been at Primrose Hall for less than a week and are already rewriting our family history? Typical."

Briar fisted her hands and moved them behind her back. She wouldn't be responsible for bruising Lord Grafton's eye again. The previous bruise was barely visible, but it was still there as a testament to her lack of self-control. Rigid with anger, Briar stood her ground and defended her romantic musings. Her voice took on a higher pitch than normal. She was thoroughly annoyed that she didn't have the ability to hide her feelings. "Typical! What do you mean?"

"It is typical for a woman such as you to make up stories and attempt to change everyone's thinking on a situation."

"A woman such as I?"

"An American."

There it was again. His disdain for her nationality. She was half British, but reminding him of this would not win the argument. "You are the most insufferable man I have ever had the displeasure of speaking with." She turned to leave but stopped as she had the overwhelming desire for him to agree with her about the first Earl of Grafton. "The earl and countess may have married for duty, but I choose to believe love won out in the end."

"You choose to believe your version of their lives and ignore the truth? However do you manage to live each day with such inaccurate convictions?"

"Inaccurate?" Briar squeaked. She needed to come up with something better to say, otherwise he would make her look the fool. She stumbled over a few broken sentences unable to decide on the worst insult for the wretched man.

Instead of giving her time to think, Lord Grafton laughed at her. He was enjoying himself at her expense. "When you decide on the best insult, you will find me in the den." Lord Grafton gave her a curt nod and stepped toward the door.

As her tongue loosened, Briar spoke barely above a whisper. "You are a wicked, wicked, and awful man."

He stopped his exit and turned toward her. "Never in my life have I been told as much. I will take your assessment under advisement." Lord Grafton again turned so he could leave her in the gallery, but she was not going to allow him to have the last word.

Forcing her feet forward, Briar quickened her pace so she could be the first to exit the room. When she realized Lord Grafton was in a foot race with her, she started running. It wasn't appropriate, her reputation was on the line, but she was determined to win. To her dismay, Lord Grafton arrived at the door before her, and then adding insult to injury he stood like a gentleman and allowed her to exit before him.

Sticking her nose firmly in the air, she chose to feign indifference.

71

But his continued laughter stirred her emotions further, and she had to make one final comment. "You did not have to be so cheeky." Briar didn't look back as Lord Grafton burst into further laughter. Her face burned with embarrassment and another emotion she didn't dare define for fear of what she would find.

Although Lord Grafton had gone out of his way to be boorish, he'd also spent more than an hour showing her around the house. Detestable men weren't inclined to do such activities. As an earl, he could have told his mother to find someone else to entertain their guest, but he hadn't. She didn't like the thoughts entering her mind, and so she decided to avoid thinking kindly about him; instead, she would make an extra effort to vex him.

Chapter Twelve

Baxter was thankful that Gigi had taken charge of their houseguest. He hadn't any idea how to entertain a woman. Miss Kensington was turning out to be exactly what he'd expected from an American who lacked proper breeding, or so he constantly bemoaned to himself as he tried to remove her from his mind. He didn't want to think about her, yet his thoughts seemed to focus on Miss Kensington no matter what he did.

He needed to clear his mind of the woman, if only to save his sanity. And so he tried to avoid her when possible. Yet, he saw her during meals and after-supper conversation. When he couldn't remove her from his thoughts, he planned to rely on his brothers and Gigi for a buffer as he didn't understand what was happening to him. He'd never been so unnerved by a woman in all his life, and he didn't know why she affected him so. Her behavior during the house tour should have been enough to keep his mind elsewhere, but in truth, he'd enjoyed the banter. The little foot race before she called him cheeky had been surprisingly fun.

He would never admit to Miss Kensington that he found her romantic notions about the first earl favorable. He'd never taken the time to read the journals that lay buried within the shelves of the library. The convictions Miss Kensington had regarding the relationship of the first earl and countess were pleasant and added to the beauty of the ruins he loved so much.

After doing a poor job of showing her the house, he sequestered himself in the library. He thought about reading the journals of the second earl, but deep down he wanted to share the experience with Miss Kensington. It was a confusing desire, and so he chose to push the emotions away. He ignored the leather-bound journals sitting on the shelf and focused on reading about crops and estate management.

For the first few weeks of her visit, Baxter's life hadn't changed from his regular routine. He had been able to ignore his houseguest and the confusing emotions of having her so nearby. He'd purposefully ignored his brothers fawning over her, yet he secretly feared one of them would form an attachment and request her hand in marriage. He'd done all he could to ignore the inkling of interest bubbling inside until he saw Miss Kensington in a dark blue party gown with her hair perfectly positioned atop her head. Gigi had gone out of her way to make Miss Kensington more than presentable in a new dress with the latest London fashion and new slippers. He had also heard his mother's abigail had spent hours on Miss Kensington's hair.

As he stood in the drawing room listening to Mr. Hayes and Archie speak of the latest news from London, Baxter's attention was drawn to his mother and Miss Kensington. Gigi's goal was to introduce Miss Kensington to all the eligible gentlemen. If anyone asked, Baxter would claim he desired her gone from his protection. But the angst of being near her told him he would miss her bold personality and the contradiction she offered to his staunch convictions.

In his confusion of wanting to be near her and despising everything her American upbringing lacked, he had to admit she was lovely, and he couldn't continue disliking her. Her hair was dark brown, but when the light from a candle in a wall sconce shone down upon her head, he was certain streaks of red peeked through. When she blushed, the pounding of his heart convinced him no woman had ever looked so innocent and attractive. He didn't want to admire her, and the warring nature of his heart and mind left him staring at the woman wishing his duty wouldn't prohibit a courtship.

"Baxter, have you heard a word we have said?" Archie made a show of looking in the direction Baxter was focused, which made Baxter cringe. He didn't need his brother making assumptions. "Ah... I see."

"I was distracted. What were you speaking about?" Baxter hoped Archie would forget about his wistful focus on Miss Kensington and repeat the important parts of the conversation.

"We are discussing the latest scandal regarding Lord Byron and Lady Caroline Lamb, but I have a feeling the gossip here is better."

"Oh, you know I pay no heed to gossip."

Hayes in his bright orange pantaloons and pink waistcoat looked affronted. Thankfully, he'd completely missed Archie's hint about Miss Kensington. "However do you manage to live with such a boring brother, Archie? I do declare Lord Grafton believes the finer points of Society to be beneath his notice."

Baxter didn't care for the trumped-up frivolities of Society's fops, but Hayes had long been a friend of the family, and he was used to the ridiculous behavior of their neighbor. Instead of engaging in the banter, Baxter turned his attention back to Miss Kensington and Gigi. He wanted to know who his mother had introduced her to.

Each smile in Miss Kensington's direction somehow put a dagger in his heart. His chest tightened as men he knew to be perfectly acceptable matches would smile and speak to Miss Kensington. He should be happy to see so many people liked her. Her grandfather had requested Baxter help find Miss Kensington a match, yet he now regretted agreeing to the arrangement. Matching her with anyone would be difficult, if not heartbreaking, for him.

As Gigi escorted Miss Kensington to their circle, Baxter looked back to his brother and Mr. Hayes to find out where the conversation had landed. He didn't want Miss Kensington to think he was a gossip, nor did he want Archie to mention anything about Baxter's watchful eye. He feared she would find him impertinent and then she could add "lout" to the list of the qualities she'd assigned to him: wicked, odious, and cheeky. As he realized he wanted her good opinion, Baxter pushed the thought aside. Her good opinion wasn't necessary, and he shouldn't spend time dwelling on it. She'd wormed her way into his affections with her audacious attitude, but since he needed to find a proper British wife, he would rid his mind of the American.

He decided it would be best to describe the attraction he felt as temporary. Love at first sight was not possible and was only found in fairy tales. He hated to consider his feelings as lust, but it was a better term than love. He thought she was pretty, and that was all. There were better matches for him, and he would find a woman who'd been bred to hold the title of countess.

"Such a disastrous end to the affair. No one could have imagined he'd end it so soon. I do not think Lady Caroline will ever recover." Hayes tended to make himself sound like the connoisseur of all things, especially gossip. The more dramatic the scandal, the more he spoke about it.

Baxter cleared his throat to warn Hayes and Archie of the additional listeners. When Mr. Hayes didn't take the hint, Baxter spoke over the man. It wouldn't be appropriate for Miss Kensington and Gigi to hear about such depravity, although he did long to see Miss Kensington's cheeks in a rosy hue again. Baxter sighed. Such errant thoughts weren't helpful.

"Mr. Hayes, I do not think you have met our delightful new neighbor, Miss Kensington." Baxter prided himself on making the introduction with as little emotion as possible. He needed to appear unaffected by Miss Kensington and her enchanting brown eyes and saucy responses to everything he said.

"It is my pleasure." Mr. Hayes bowed over Miss Kensington's hand and made a show of the entire introduction. "Miss Kensington, what do you think of the sordid situation with Lord Byron and Lady Caroline?"

"I have not received an introduction to either of them, and therefore, it would be inappropriate for me to form an opinion worth sharing."

Baxter appreciated her response, and against his desires to push her away, his estimation for her grew. He had rightfully assumed she wasn't the type of woman to engage in gossip. All of England had been scandalized by the affair, and it was refreshing to find she didn't want to engage in the topic.

"You are an American?" Hayes said, noting her accent by wiggling his fingers in front of her mouth. "I had heard Kensington's long-lost granddaughter was supposed to arrive. I am glad you are here."

"Thank you, sir."

"Miss Kensington, what have you enjoyed most about Yorkshire so far?"

"I have not had a chance to see much, since it has been snowing so often. But I have a perfectly lovely view of the ruins, and I think they will forever be my favorite part of Yorkshire."

Mr. Hayes bounced on his feet in excitement. "Miss Kensington, did you know the ruins are haunted?"

Archie interjected before Baxter could refute Hayes's claim. "They are not, Miss Kensington. Do not believe a word he says about ghosts and ghouls."

While Hayes and Archie debated, Baxter mulled over the intrusion of Miss Kensington on his ruins. She was far too preoccupied with the history of that edifice. He needed to find a way to dissuade her from searching them out. Since his father's death, Baxter had taken to spending time there. Other than the library and his den, it was a place he could think and sort through the stress of his responsibilities. If she were to invade his sanctuary, he'd never find peace again. Even the thought of her standing upon the steps leading up to the tower made his heart pound in his chest.

Baxter took a moment to chide himself for the ridiculous turn his thoughts had taken. He didn't want to be friends with Miss Kensington. Logically he didn't want anything to do with her, and yet his mind and heart would not agree upon the decision to like or dislike the woman. As he tried to stop the images of Miss Kensington in his ruins from filling his mind, he realized his eyes were focused on her smile. Her lips were perfectly formed, with a little crease in the middle, and he wanted nothing more than to take her to the ruins and walk with her upon the tower walls, and—

"Miss Kensington, if you will allow me to show you the ruins tomorrow, I will escort you in my carriage." Hayes's voice broke through Baxter's thoughts.

He had to do something to stop the invasion. No matter how inadvisable and foolish it was, he would be the one to share the ruins with Miss Kensington. Heart pounding and fists clenched, he was anxious to keep his place of peace to himself until he was ready to share it with her, but he had to earn her trust first. Baxter blurted out the only excuse he could think of to keep them from going to the ruins. "It is not safe to travel there. The snow is deep up on the hill, and there is a lot of ice, which has made the stones dangerous. Your carriage will be stuck in the snow and mud until spring if you attempt it."

Hayes looked shocked by Baxter's outburst, but he conceded the point. "Then we will have to go in the spring."

Baxter hoped that Miss Kensington would be gone from Yorkshire before spring. He didn't want the memory of her walking along the cobblestone pathway into the ruins to haunt his solitude. A match with Miss Kensington wasn't possible, and no matter how attractive she was, he could not forget his duty as her protector. He stood silently, listening to the conversation as he battled the emotions raging through his chest. This sudden attraction to Miss Kensington would be easily forgotten once he focused his mind and set about his duties on his estate. He swiftly reminded himself that duty and honor were more important than giving into the demands of the heart.

Chapter Thirteen

Almost everyone was kind—even Lord Grafton kept a civil tongue for the evening—and the party seemed perfect. Their hosts were Mr. and Mrs. Stillman. Mrs. Stillman had a dress of the finest pink silk muslin Briar had ever seen. As it was winter, she hadn't expected anyone to dress so insensibly. The gown looked more like a summer gown with its wide neckline and the low plunging back. It wasn't surprising to see that Mrs. Stillman spent her evening standing close to the fire.

Remembering her grandfather's request that she find herself a match, Briar had set about the task hoping to gain favor with at least one man. She'd paid attention to conversations but found each of them wanting. In fact, the only man who stood out to her was the one with the audacity to dress like a peacock.

Briar couldn't claim she hadn't enjoyed herself, but there was something lacking in her evening. She'd danced with several men, all of whom had been nice. Conversations were pleasant but nothing notable. In truth, Briar missed her parents and her grandfather. She knew it wasn't possible to have her parents there, but she wished her grandfather could have been the one guiding her around the party and making introductions. He would have been able to point out the acceptable men, men who wouldn't be offended by her American upbringing and her family's fortune being made through hard work and industry.

If there was one thing she'd learned since stepping foot on British soil, it was that gentlemen shouldn't have professions. Men from the upper ten-thousand were snobs, and the women were far worse. Even the Society of Yorkshire frowned upon a self-made man, and with a few of the polite snubs she'd received that night, she understood her grandfather to be respected but not accepted by all. It was possible some only tolerated his presence because of his wealth.

"Lady Grafton, I do not know if I will remember everyone's names." She'd met so many people, she was bound to forget most of them. She'd also purposefully written off a few of the people as unnecessary acquaintances; unfortunately, their names sat at the forefront of her mind.

"I will be by your side to help you remember." Lady Grafton patted her hand while she searched for newcomers they hadn't yet spoken with. "You should call me Gigi. All of my sons do."

"I had noticed the term. Why do they call you that?"

"When Baxter was very young, he misunderstood my Christian name and called me Gigi instead. I have been known—only to my children—as Gigi ever since then."

Briar knew Christian names were very rarely used amongst the *ton*, but she was curious to know how a name could be misunderstood so thoroughly. "May I inquire as to your Christian name?"

"Georgiana. You can see where the mistake was made."

"Yes. And only your children call you Gigi? Are you certain you want me to be so informal?"

"Yes, I feel as though you are a daughter to me."

So many emotions went through Briar with that simple statement. She liked Lady Grafton and thought her to be a wonderful friend, and there had been moments where she'd felt a motherly love from the woman, but a surrogate mother was a position she'd never expected to bestow upon anyone. She didn't want to replace her mother.

"Thank you." She needed to say something, and a party wasn't the time to become melancholy over a loss. If she didn't guard her emotions, she would start crying and find herself embarrassed.

"My late husband also called me Gigi, but only in the privacy of our home. He was much like Baxter when it came to Society. He tried to be the perfect gentleman." Gigi's nostalgic tone left Briar wishing she hadn't asked such personal questions. "He was, by all accounts, a man worth emulating."

"I wish I had known him. It might have helped me to understand the current Lord Grafton."

Gigi continued patting her hand, but she stopped looking around the room and focused on Briar. A smile that said much more than pleasure crossed her face. "Baxter is learning how to be an earl. Everything he has been taught to this point in life is now pressing down upon his shoulders. Do not judge him too harshly, at least not right now."

Briar felt the sting of rebuke, and she nodded. "I promise to reevaluate my interactions with him. I will try to be less argumentative."

"You misunderstand me, I have enjoyed seeing the challenge you have brought to my son. He needs someone to let him know when he has made himself look the fool. But do not become discouraged by his need for order. Baxter will find his way, but we must give him time."

"Lord Grafton is so different from your other sons." She didn't want to admit he was the most admirable out of them, so she left her comment where it sat.

"Yes, but they all have their individual talents. The more time you spend at Primrose Hall, the more you will see this is true. Now, what did you think of Mr. Hayes?"

"The man with the orange pantaloons?"

"Yes, he is eccentric but very good company. We invite him to dine at Primrose Hall often."

"He did seem very nice." She wasn't certain what to say. He had been overly excited about everything she said, especially about the ruins. He did seem like a nice man, but would she tire of his constant need for chatter? He'd hardly taken a breath while she'd been near him, and he'd nearly spoken over Lord Grafton when he tried to make a comment.

"Mr. Hayes and my second eldest son, Archie, are good friends." Briar stayed silent, as Gigi seemed to be caught up in a memory. "I think Mr. Hayes took notice of you. I will not be surprised if he visits in the morning."

Briar's eyes went wide. "I had not considered Mr. Hayes a suitable match. He is so peculiar."

"You are the correct age for a marriage. You will not want to wait too long, otherwise you will be considered on the shelf."

"Do you think I should consider Mr. Hayes for courtship?"

"If he decides to call on you, yes. You should give him a chance, and then perhaps the right man will emerge."

Briar looked over at the group of men and focused on Mr. Hayes. She might be able to overlook his poor sense of fashion if Gigi declared him a fine gentleman. "What do you mean?"

"If you make yourself available, then I believe the man who is your perfect match will take notice and ask for your hand."

"Then you think Mr. Hayes is not suitable, but he will lead me to the right match?" Briar was very confused. It seemed wrong to use Mr. Hayes in such a manner.

Gigi went back to patting Briar's hand. "He could be the right man. You will not know unless you allow for his visits."

Briar stood in confusion, wondering what Gigi had meant. She spent the rest of the evening contemplating the cryptic message that must be hidden within Gigi's words. By the time the party was over, she hadn't any idea what to think of Gigi or Yorkshire Society.

As Briar readied for bed that night, she allowed her eyes to glaze over in concentration as her maid pulled pins out of Briar's coiffeur. Mr. Hayes was the most curious out of all the men she'd met, with his vibrant clothing and talkative personality. Lord Grafton was the complete opposite and had portrayed the usual grumpy earl persona he was so intent on keeping. But even with those two men, Briar found a small amount of familiarity in Yorkshire Society. She could compare most of the partygoers to friends and acquaintances in Boston. Although they spoke with an accent, their concerns were much the same as those so far away. They spoke of family, friends, and social gatherings, which was exactly what she would have chatted about if she'd been in one of the finest homes in Boston.

RIDING WAS ONE OF BRIAR'S FAVORITE PASTIMES, AND SHE was thankful her grandfather had gifted her a horse. Although Lord Grafton had a large stable full of mares, she would prefer to walk for exercise over asking the detestable man for anything. Thankful her grandfather had seen fit to send her horse, Glory, to the stables at Primrose Hall, Briar dressed in her emerald riding habit and requested her mare be prepared for exercise.

"Miss Kensington, will you allow Mr. Hayes and me to accompany you on your ride?" Archie asked.

She had no reason to turn them away, so she stood by the paddock waiting until their horses were prepared. Remembering her grandfather's hope that she would match with one of the Fernley men, Briar took a moment to consider Archibald Fernley. He was a writer, and for his craft, he spent an inordinate amount of time analyzing people. She wondered what he thought of her and if he would use her for one of his stories.

Archie, as he'd asked her to call him, always wore a pleasant smile on his face. Tilting her head to the side to examine him more fully, she noticed the spine of a notebook and a stick peeking out of his coat pocket. She knew it was a graphite pencil. It was common to see him jotting down notes, especially during emotional moments. In the short time she'd been at Primrose Hall, she'd noticed Archie had more imagination than his brothers. This made him a good fit for friendship with Mr. Hayes, but not a match for her.

She didn't know the exact qualities she was searching for when it came to a future husband. She knew a man who could provide a suitable living would be best, and she feared Archie would need a woman's dowry to sustain his lifestyle. With proper management, they could live comfortably, but the example of her father and grandfather as businessmen made her think that was what she wanted. She would become bored with a man who stared at a spider for hours on end as it crawled along the wall so he could describe the movements in detail along with all eight hairy legs.

Mr. Hayes had been on her mind since meeting him the previous night. He'd taken the morning meal with the family, which meant he'd arrived early for a visit. She'd noticed he'd chatted, smiled at the right moments, and engaged her in conversation when appropriate. Gigi had been right when she'd said he admired Briar, and although it was pleasing, she wasn't certain if she wanted the man to pursue her. She would prefer a man who dressed less obviously.

If she had to choose a husband in that very moment, she would choose neither Archie nor Mr. Hayes. Allowing her mind to consider the men of Yorkshire, her thoughts filled with an overly starched white cravat tightly knotted at the neck, a double-breasted gold satin waistcoat, brown jacket with M-shaped lapels, beige pantaloons, and pristinely polished Hessian boots. As Lord Grafton's stern countenance filled her mind, she shook her head, hoping to rid her thoughts of the man. She didn't want him to court her, and she didn't care to gain the odious man's good opinion.

Thankfully, for her, Lord Grafton was out of her reach, and being the detestable man that he was, she truly wouldn't want him anyway. She would not allow her heart to pine after a man for his handsome features and sensible choices in fashion, for she was certain her attraction to him was completely physical. There was nothing about his character worth knowing.

"Are you ready?" Mr. Hayes asked, pulling Briar out of her thoughts. "Your eyes looked far away. Were you thinking of Boston?"

She blushed, knowing a confession of her internal debate would be inappropriate, but she also couldn't lead them to believe she'd been thinking of home. "I was thinking about all of the people I have met since arriving in Yorkshire." It wasn't a complete lie, but it saved her the embarrassment of letting them know she was trying to decide if either of them would be a suitable match.

Briar allowed Mr. Hayes to assist her in mounting the horse, and then they slowly left the yard. As they rode, Briar looked to the familiar ruins, wishing she could spend her day walking through the old stone fortress. The walls were still standing, at least on the side she could see. A tower hovered high above the outer walls, eroding with the temperament of nature. Slivers of sunlight accentuated the moss creeping between the bricks as if they held each one firmly in place.

Hoping to one day climb to the top of the tower, Briar's eye caught movement. She squinted and narrowed her gaze to see it was a man walking along the top of the wall. "I thought Lord Grafton said the ruins are too dangerous for a visit this time of year."

Archie and Mr. Hayes both turned their attention to see where she pointed. When Archie spoke, his words left Briar in a state of unrest. "Baxter follows his own set of rules."

"Do you mean to tell me the dolt walking upon the wall is Lord Grafton?" She'd thought it was someone with less sense than the earl, and then she regretted considering the earl as a sensible man. He was infuriating. "He will not allow visitors to the ruins, but he will climb about the walls in an effort to taunt my curiosity?"

Lord Grafton had no way of knowing she could see him. When he'd taken to the ruins, he'd probably given it little thought. But Briar loved the gothic romantic nature of the building, and Lord Grafton had prohibited her from exploring the edifice. A familiar heaviness settled upon her chest; she would punish the man for his insolence.

Archie defended his brother, which she had expected. No one ever spoke ill of the earl. His brothers and Gigi adored him, as did everyone from the night before. It nearly made her sick to think of all the complimentary claims they'd bestowed upon her aching brain throughout the party. "Baxter told you the truth, it is dangerous to go up there this time of year. But it does not stop him from attempting to break his neck."

Briar continued to look at the figure on the top of the wall. He'd not only gone up to the ruins, but he'd climbed to the tallest of the stone walls and was now sitting and looking out over his estate. Her soul yearned to be next to him with her legs dangling over the edge of the walls. She didn't have to speak to the disagreeable man, she only wanted to look out upon the open fields and see the beauty of Yorkshire.

"It cannot be too dangerous if Lord Grafton is there. Why can we not ride over and climb the walls as well?" She hoped the men would agree and show her the fastest path. If she was persuasive enough, they might give in.

Mr. Hayes moved his horse to block her from turning in the direction of the ruins as though he'd read her every thought. "Miss Kensington, everyone at Primrose Hall, and I include myself in this statement, desires your safety. If the current Lord Grafton falls from the top of the tower, it will be a very devastating loss, but Archie will inherit the title and life will resume as normal. We do not have another Miss Kensington to replace you."

She knew he'd meant it to be kind, a way to persuade her to listen to their advice and stay away from the ruins, but he sounded callous and ridiculous. "It would be terrible to lose anyone in such a manner. His title would pass to Archie, yes, but the current Lord Grafton would be sorely missed."

Archie nodded his appreciation. "Well said, Miss Kensington. Next time you are sparring with my brother, I will remind you of this moment."

Briar blushed. She could feel the heat in her cheeks as she imagined Lord Grafton's utter astonishment over her defense of his life. He would never let her forget such an errant comment, and although she'd meant every word, she couldn't allow him to know she spared a thought for his safety. He might misinterpret her concern and then they'd have another awkward argument followed by her embarrassment. "Please, do not tell him anything. I fear he will never let me win another argument."

"Have you won any yet?"

"I do believe I have." She wouldn't tell Archie which of the arguments she counted as a triumph. Allowing anyone to believe Lord Grafton had won every verbal spar with her was ludicrous. As she rode next to both her escorts, Briar decided she would find the right time to confront Lord Grafton over the ruins. He'd purposefully kept her away from them by claiming they were dangerous. She would prove him to be a deceitful man. And by doing so, she would find her way to the top of the ruins, as she'd planned from the moment she'd become obsessed with the history and people of that place.

Chapter Fourteen

Baxter sat at his desk reviewing the estate ledgers. He hated this part of his life. Running an estate would be simpler if he didn't have to check over the accountant's sums each month. But his father had told him horror stories of men wealthier than he who had lost their wealth by trusting the wrong advisors and accountants. Baxter had been taught that an earl should always take part in every facet of the estate. This meant to fulfill his duty and preserve the title and estate for future generations, he had to review the finances.

As he matched bills and receipts to line items, Baxter double-checked each sum. His esteem for the accountant grew as he confirmed the man was trustworthy. It relieved a bit of his burden each month to know the people he employed were honest and good.

"My lord?" Ames approached the desk and held out a sliver tray. A card on fancy, bright-pink stationary sat in the middle upon an embroidered cloth.

Looking down at the card, Baxter's interest was piqued. He'd seen the card many times and didn't have to pick it up to know it was their flamboyant fop of a neighbor. "Mr. Hayes is here to see me?"

"No, my lord. He is here to call upon Miss Kensington. Lady Grafton has requested you join them in the morning room."

"Twice in one week? Has the man no shame?"

"I can honestly say I do not think shame has ever been a problem for Mr. Hayes, my lord." Ames kept a straight face as he made his statement, which made Baxter smile. His stalwart butler rarely ventured out of propriety, but when he did, it was generally to show his disapproval of Mr. Hayes's behavior.

"You are right, Ames. I should never have questioned Hayes's intentions." Baxter chuckled so Ames would know he appreciated the witty comment. Knowing his mother was concerned about propriety, Baxter closed the ledger. "Will you put this away?"

"Yes, my lord."

As he entered the parlor, Baxter greeted the occupants and took a seat near the window. He would stay in the room for the entire visit, but it didn't mean he needed to engage in conversation while Mr. Hayes attempted to flirt with Miss Kensington.

He'd been unsettled since the night of the party, but when thoughts of Miss Kensington started haunting his waking hours, Baxter knew he had to push them aside for the sake of propriety. As part of this effort, he had decided an aloof attitude would suffice. If he stayed away from her, there would be nothing to think about, and before long, he'd forget about her porcelain features, deep brown eyes, and cheeky attitude. He decided to use the time to rest his eyes, but his insensible heart wouldn't allow him to ignore the conversation.

"Miss Kensington, do you plan to spend any time in London during the spring? The London season is the place to be for any woman of marriageable age."

"I am at the mercy of my hosts. I have not heard if they will attend the season."

Baxter grumbled internally. Realizing all the differences in how she interacted with him versus Mr. Hayes was one more way for him

90

to push her from his mind. Miss Kensington spoke with such sweetness. He'd never been on the receiving end of a pretty conversation and a sweet smile with her. As he thought the words, a nagging voice inside his head tried to convince him it was his fault she'd reacted with sass to everything he said.

"Grafton, will you set out for London this spring?" It wasn't surprising to hear Hayes yell across the room. He paid little heed to rules of etiquette when in a comfortable place.

"I had not planned to find myself in London until next fall."

"Do not tell me you will keep this delightful creature hidden away. Miss Kensington should take part in the upper circles of Society."

Delightful was the word Baxter had used to describe Miss Kensington at the party. He didn't think Hayes was using the word appropriately, especially with his exaggerated tones and pink polka dot cravat.

Miss Kensington laughed and shook her head playfully, which caused Baxter's jealousy to flare. Baxter had known debutantes schooled in the art of flirting, but none of them were as talented as the woman sitting across the room. Every movement she made sent a longing through him. He knew what she was doing, yet he was intrigued. He had to constantly remind himself that she was an American and he didn't want her. He wanted a proper British woman, and so he needed to get his mind straightened out and stop admiring this traitor to the crown.

"Mr. Hayes, your shameful compliments have not gone unnoticed. Thank you for the kind words, but I have it on good authority that an uncultured American has no place in high British Society." Miss Kensington looked in his direction as she said the latter part of her statement. There was no humor in her features, and Baxter hated that she'd somehow known exactly what he'd been thinking.

An unspoken challenge had been issued. He was certain she planned to goad him into an argument. If he was correct, it would

91

mean she truly didn't enjoy Mr. Hayes's company. If she wasn't and he'd misunderstood her meaning, he would look foolish. He decided she must not admire Hayes, and therefore he would leave her to the flirtation. He wouldn't take the bait and show himself to be a jealous man. She had made her choice to flirt with Hayes, and she would have to suffer the consequences of his courtship.

Satisfied that he now understood the wiles of Briar Kensington, Baxter chose to rest his head against the back of the chair and close his eyes. His mind wandered to the first time he'd met Miss Kensington. He regretted his behavior then, and even more, he found dissatisfaction in the staunch conviction he had in loyalty to king and country, but it was who he was. He couldn't betray his king by consorting with an American. Not in the king's current state of insanity.

Baxter sighed. He was being ridiculous, and he knew it. There was no law prohibiting him from marrying an American. It happened all the time, and moreover, men in high society married women from France and other countries. More than one duke, marquess, and earl had been known to marry a wealthy heiress to sustain his extravagant lifestyle. Even the king had married a woman from outside of British society; Queen Charlotte was from Germany. So why did Baxter oppose Miss Kensington?

Baxter nearly grunted his confusion out loud, but he stopped himself as he heard Miss Kensington and Mr. Hayes laugh. Their flirting enraged the green-eyed monster of jealousy, and he had to either leave the room or stop the conversation. Since he didn't want to be attracted to the woman, his emotions were irrational. Baxter took a calming breath and tried to analyze the situation. What was happening to his calm demeanor? Why was he bothered by this woman who was merely a guest and under his protection? He didn't care for her. Even as he thought the words, he knew it wasn't true. He cared far more than he was ready to admit.

"What wretch would say such a terrible thing to you?" Mr.

Hayes asked, his voice high pitched in stunned disbelief. "I know at least one family that would find you a most excellent guest."

Baxter chuckled internally. If Hayes only knew of one family that would enjoy Miss Kensington's company, then it wasn't much of a compliment. As Baxter considered the slight toward Miss Kensington, he realized as her protector that it was something he needed to correct. As a man confused over his feelings for the woman, he wanted to rip Mr. Hayes's eyes out and send the fop running from Primrose Hall. As it would be cruel and inappropriate to treat Mr. Hayes so badly, Baxter decided to ignore the latter and defend Miss Kensington's honor with propriety.

Miss Kensington spoke before Baxter could censure Hayes for his callous remark. "I do believe wretch is the proper term for the man. Why, only the other night he claimed the ruins were dangerous, but I saw him climbing upon the outer walls without a care for the ice and snow."

The cutting remark about his character nearly forced a smile onto his face. He decided her continued banter toward him was a way of gaining his attention. It made him feel justified in his admiration to think that she was trying to flirt with him instead of Hayes.

Baxter kept his face straight as he cleared his throat before speaking. With all eyes in the room on him, he censured Hayes for his rude remark. "I dare say, Mr. Hayes, if you can only find one family to host an evening's entertainment for Miss Kensington, the season will be beneath her notice."

Mr. Hayes instantly sat forward. "I did not mean to say there would only be one party to attend. My statement was clearly out of accord with my thoughts. I do apologize for the unintended insult."

"You are forgiven, Mr. Hayes." Miss Kensington gave Hayes a genuine smile, which left Baxter baffled and wishing she'd smiled at him in gratitude for defending her honor. Her mistreatment of him was truly horrific.

"From the very moment we met, I knew you would be the most magnanimous of all my acquaintances," Mr. Hayes crooned.

"You are too kind, Mr. Hayes. Tell me, where did you learn your sense of fashion?"

Once they'd moved onto a conversation regarding muslin, silks, cotton, and other materials, Baxter allowed his mind to focus on the intricacies of women and everything he didn't know about them. The one thing he was certain of, above all else, was that the female mind was a complicated mystery he did not know how to solve.

Focused so intently on his thoughts, Baxter didn't realize he was dozing in the chair until Gilbert touched his shoulder. "Baxter, you are needed in town."

Instantly aware of his duty, Baxter stood and ignored the desire to go to his bedchamber and crawl into bed. He was mentally worn out. "What has happened?"

"Mr. Craig has arrested Daniel Vanstone for theft."

Baxter was thankful everyone in the family, including the servants, knew what to do in these moments. Ames held Baxter's gloves, coat, and hat. One of the footmen was sent to the stables, and Gigi was informing Mr. Hayes that his flirting session with Miss Kensington was over. His household ran smoothly, allowing him to perform his duties with ease.

"What is he accused of stealing?" Baxter asked as he slipped his hand in one of the gloves.

"Mrs. Walsh had a mince pie resting on the window, and it is gone. They believe Daniel took it."

"Is there any proof?"

"The pie is gone, other than the stains on Daniel's trousers."

Baxter groaned. This wasn't the first time Daniel had been caught stealing food. In the past, Baxter had been able to sentence him to labor at a local farm, which allowed Daniel to work off his debt. Another infraction would mean a stint in the workhouse.

"I do not envy your position," Gigi said as she secured Baxter's coat to keep him warm.

"I warned Vanstone the last time he stood before me that it would mean the workhouse. I do not understand why he stole again."

"You would sentence a man to the workhouse for stealing food? Perhaps he was starving." Miss Kensington stood by the wall, her face contorted in concern for a man she didn't know.

For a moment, Baxter lost his senses and wondered why he was planning to leave the house in a snowstorm to convict a man of a crime. Miss Kensington made him question everything he knew. He took a moment to gather his wits. Baxter nodded his head. "I have a duty to the people of this town and the surrounding hamlets. As magistrate, I must uphold the law."

"Why would you do that? What if he had no food? When was the last time he ate?" Baxter feared tears would fall from her fragile eyes onto her pink porcelain cheeks as she innocently questioned him. He wouldn't know what to do if the woman became hysterical. Would Gigi know how to calm her?

"He was given a position on a local farm the last time he stole food. He was warned never to do so again, otherwise there would be further consequences." The reasoning was logical to him, but it must not have made any sense to Miss Kensington, because she continued to stare at him as though he were speaking a foreign language. "What would you have me do? Release him and allow him to continue stealing from people who work hard for everything they have?"

"No, I would not. But I would ask you to consider that not everyone has the same privileges as you do, my lord. Have compassion upon the man and see if there is a better way to help him than to imprison him."

"He has multiple offenses. I cannot be lenient."

The erstwhile fragility in her eyes was replaced with fire. "I certainly hope one day you do not meet with such an unfeeling judge content to uphold the law instead of offering mercy. If it appeases Mrs. Walsh, I will pay for the ingredients she lost so the man can go free."

Baxter didn't want to argue with Miss Kensington, but she needed to understand that he wasn't an unfeeling wretch. He'd given Daniel Vanstone a chance to make a life for himself, but he had chosen a life of petty theft instead. The laws of the land were not subject to the whims of the people, at least not in England. "It may be the practice in America to allow criminals to roam free thieving from innocent hardworking people, but it is not the way for a country with laws and order."

He didn't wait for her response. Instead, Baxter turned away and stormed out of the house. As he mounted his horse, he replayed the scene from the house and all the various ways he could have responded. He could have explained his decision with kindness, and yet he'd instantly chosen an unbending reply. As a guest in his home, she didn't have the right to question his duty.

"She was trying to understand. There was no reason to speak harshly," Gilbert said. Filled with frustration over the conversation with Miss Kensington, Baxter had forgotten his brother was riding next to him.

"She should not have questioned my position. If I do not send Vanstone to the workhouse, then I should retire my position as magistrate. I must ensure the safety of those in my care. I cannot allow someone to continuously steal from others. Mrs. Walsh is a widow and has a small annuity. She cannot feed thieves."

"I agree."

"Your words make sense, but the hesitation in your voice leads me to believe you have more to say on the matter."

Gilbert didn't speak immediately, which didn't surprise Baxter. It was one of Gilbert's strengths that he examined each situation and offered suggestions for improvement or resolution. While he waited for Gilbert to respond, Baxter ignored the regret for his harsh reply to

Miss Kensington and took in the beauty of the falling snow. The snowflakes fell clumped together and landed on the brim of his hat like tiny balls of wool. As each flake landed, they clung to the bushes and trees, leaving the world around him in a fresh white layer of frozen coldness. It was far too indicative of his current feelings toward Miss Kensington. She left him in a severe state of unrest where he questioned himself and his duty.

"You cannot let Daniel's crime go unpunished. Even the scriptures tell us that vengeance should be swift." Baxter was thankful when Gilbert left off the part where the scriptures say that vengeance belonged to God. As magistrate, he had to enforce the law. "Is it possible to give him the minimum sentence?"

Baxter had already decided Daniel Vanstone would serve six months in the workhouse. He hoped it would give the man a taste of what awaited if he was brought before the court again for thievery. "I am not concerned about the judgement I will place upon Daniel. My biggest worry at this moment is Miss Kensington. How do I respond when she finds out I sentenced Daniel to the workhouse?" Even as the words left his mouth, Baxter knew he'd accepted the shocking revelation his heart had been forcing upon him. He cared about Miss Kensington, and he yearned to have her good opinion.

"Let us hope Gigi is explaining your position as magistrate to Miss Kensington. By the time you arrive home, she will be perfectly happy and will no longer question your judicial decisions."

Baxter laughed, but only because he didn't want to groan. Miss Kensington would not be easy to persuade on the matter. He'd seen the challenge in her eyes as flames had danced upon her cheeks. He was certain she would have more to say on the subject, and deep down, he was looking forward to the verbal sparring.

Chapter Fifteen

Briar had hoped to punish Lord Grafton for keeping her away from the ruins, but when he'd made Mr. Hayes apologize for the rude comment, she'd instantly forgiven him. That was until she'd discovered he held the fate of a poor man in his hands. She would never bring up her displeasure over the ruins again, but she would challenge him on his rulings as a magistrate. If a poor person stole food, they should be given work and shelter so they didn't have to steal again. Providing a poor person with the ability to care for themselves was a necessary part of offering dignity to those in unfortunate situations.

As Lord Grafton rode away, she turned to Gigi in concern. "I do not mean to question his authority, but it is not right to condemn a man when he has not the ability to feed himself."

Gigi stepped to her and pulled her toward the parlor. "Do not worry over Mr. Vanstone. Baxter is a fair man, and he will see justice is served."

"Then you agree, Mr. Vanstone must serve time in the workhouse?"

"Yes, I do. But it is not due to his financial situation."

Briar sat on the sofa and looked to Gigi for answers. "Please help me understand. At this moment, I am thinking the worst of Lord Grafton."

"The last time Mr. Vanstone was caught with food he did not purchase, Baxter gave Mr. Vanstone a job and told him if he was ever in need of food, our kitchen was open. He only needed to visit with our housekeeper, and he would have a free meal."

Heat rushed into her cheeks as she realized she had once again misjudged Lord Grafton. He wasn't the wicked unfeeling man she'd thought him to be. True, their first meeting had been horrendous, but she had carried a grudge against him he didn't fully deserve. "Why did he not say anything? Why would Lord Grafton allow me to believe him an unkind and unjust man?"

"Baxter is not one to announce the deeds of service he performs. He informed the cook, the housekeeper, and Mr. Ames of his decision to allow Mr. Vanstone food. He is unaware of my knowledge on the situation, and I will ask you not to speak to him about it."

"Why would he not want his family to know of his generosity?"

"Baxter does not seek the recognition of Society or his neighbors for the service he gives. He is content to do what he can as he considers it his duty."

"Next time I see Lord Grafton, I will apologize for my outburst." Briar left for her bedchamber to consider everything she had learned about the man who was now her protector. He was much more than a stuffy self-righteous earl. He seemed to have a heart of gold. She didn't know if she liked acknowledging his good traits because every time she was near him, she had the aching desire to force insanity upon him.

BRIAR KNEW LORD GRAFTON ENJOYED A MORNING RIDE, and so she purposefully woke early the following morning with the hope of joining him. She would speak of the delights of Boston, for it was all she truly knew well, and hope to break through his stiff temperament. If it were possible, she would help him see her finer qualities, now that she knew he was capable of more than an ornery temper and a displeasing nature.

"Sam," Briar said, as she approached the stable hand, "has Lord Grafton already left?" She noticed the empty stall at the end of the row, the one Lord Grafton's large black stallion usually occupied.

"He took Sugar Plum around the bend a moment ago, if you hurry, you can catch up to him."

"Sugar Plum?"

"Yes, miss."

She never imagined the formidable earl's horse would be named after a hard piece of candy. Tucking the information away so she could tease him about it at an appropriate time, Briar waited patiently for Sam to prepare her horse. She hadn't yet formed the exact apology she would make and needed to do so before meeting Lord Grafton along the road.

As Sam moved the mounting block into position, Briar positioned her right leg over the pommel and adjusted in her seat before setting off at a trot. She pointed Glory toward the ruins, certain Lord Grafton would go there above all other places.

As she rode, she decided she would need to be brilliantly charming. She was well liked amongst the elite of Boston. There was no reason for her reputation in England to suffer after one unfortunate meeting with an earl. Of course, she would have to change her approach and push aside all temptation to berate the man. She sighed with mock abhorrence. It would be a trial. But she also knew the friendship they could have would be worth the effort.

Glory's hooves rhythmically beat against the mud. The lack of conversation brought a contented smile to her face. She loved the peaceful, serene world around her bathed in untouched glistening snow. The silence flowed through her, rejuvenating her soul like blood coursing through her veins. This was the first time she'd been by herself since arriving at Primrose Hall. She loved Gigi and the Fernley men. They were wonderful people, and she would look upon them with fondness for the remainder of her days. But there was much to enjoy when alone. It gave her time to reflect upon her life and the direction she was taking.

Looming behind every thought, smile, and conversation was the throbbing sting of loss. The fog of tender moments where a smell could bring back a memory so intense, she was certain if she were back in Boston her parents would be sitting in the parlor of their red-brick Cambridge home waiting for her to arrive. Peppermint and lime were the worst culprits that pulled at her memories. At first, she'd thought time would heal her heart, but now she understood it wouldn't. There was no amount of time sufficient to forget the crushing heartache of losing those she loved.

An overwhelming emptiness entered Briar's soul, and she found the longing for her parents had left her emotionally exhausted. Pursuing Lord Grafton no longer seemed important nor was it necessary as she would dissolve into tears with a confrontation, and then what would Lord Grafton do? She remembered his confused fear from the day before when she'd questioned his judgement, and she knew he wouldn't appreciate another emotional encounter so soon.

Instead of searching out the earl, Briar decided she wanted to go to the church house in town and pray. She hoped Gil would allow patrons to meditate in the warmth of the chapel. With thoughts of Gil, she decided to use the time alone to analyze a possible match with him.

Gil was the local vicar, well spoken, and versed on scriptures. She respected his spirituality and found him to be thoughtful, which was a likeable quality in a man. Although he was a twin with Phineas, Gil was content to stay in Yorkshire with his family and flock. As the leader of the local vicarage, he had a responsibility to the town.

She hadn't noticed until that moment how similar and different Gil and Lord Grafton were. Lord Grafton had a duty to the town as well. As magistrate, he passed judgement upon the lawbreakers, just as Gil was able to pass a temporal judgement with spiritual ramifications. Both Lord Grafton and Gil were quiet and spent time alone with their thoughts, and yet, there was something nagging at her heart. It wasn't the unsuitability of Gil but her inability to be a vicar's wife that bothered her.

The wife of a vicar played an important role amongst the flock, and with her sassy temper, she knew she was incapable of being the woman a vicar needed. She enjoyed offering service to others, but would that be enough? Would she tire of the responsibility of being pious? There were times when she wanted to run through the fields and jump in mud puddles. A proper vicar's wife would never indulge in such activities. In her heart, she knew she had to remove another Fernley man from her list of possible suitors. When her grandfather returned, he wouldn't be happy to find she'd eliminated the entire family. But even so, she'd taken the situation seriously and was certain with Cornelius and Fletcher left to consider, she would discover if either of them suited her.

Although it was early in the morning, the familiar sounds and smells of town life filled Briar's senses. The sharp pounding of metal from the blacksmith's forge, the smell of yeast and freshly baked bread from the bakery, and smoke filling the air from the chimneys of every building in town made her happy she was there. The peaceful morning left her longing for the stillness to never end, although she did hope at some point the sun would come out and dazzle the sky with rays of warmth.

Briar was nearly to the doors of the chapel when she noticed Lord Grafton's beautiful black stallion tied to the rail. A giggle went through her as she thought of the horse's name. It spoke to all she didn't know about Lord Grafton. Sugar Plum was a name given by a child, not a grown man and especially not an earl. A man in such an important role would name his horses something serious and commanding like General, Major, or Midnight. She would have to discover the reason behind Sugar Plum's name.

Briar still wanted to ponder and pray in the church, but her curiosity was piqued, and her eagerness to know what Lord Grafton was doing in town won out. Did Lord Grafton frequent the church? The vicar was his brother, so it was possible they had family business to discuss. Or was Lord Grafton a praying man? She didn't know much about her elusive protector because he kept his distance, but she wondered what lay beneath his poised exterior.

Dismounting, Briar pulled Glory to the opposite side of the road and led him behind the local haberdashery. She tied the reins to a post and slowly made her way through the snow to sneak a peek in the church window. As she crouched low to not be seen, Briar stopped, and then screamed as a pair of black boots with legs inside them stepped in front of her path.

"Miss Kensington, you will wake all of Yorkshire with such a loud cry." Lord Grafton's amused smile with his firm jawline bothered her. His eyes were narrowed with suspicion, but his lips twitched as he held back a laugh.

"You gave me a fright, my lord."

"I apologize. It was not my intention."

Briar realized she was still crouching low, so she stood to her full height. "If you will excuse me, I'll continue with my previous plans."

Lord Grafton quirked an eyebrow in curiosity. "You still plan to sneak around the churchyard?"

Folding her arms over her stomach, Briar glared at Lord Grafton. He knew the answer to his impertinent question. Need she truly respond? "I most certainly do not. Whatever gave you such a ridiculous notion?"

Grafton held out his hands and pointed to her and then the

window. "I did catch you in a very unladylike crouch. Either you are planning to spy on the vicar, or you are searching for spiders."

"Spiders?" Briar instantly looked to the ground to make certain she wasn't standing near the hairy eight-legged creatures or their webs.

"I see, then it was my brother you plan to spy on. Gilbert will find it thoroughly entertaining to know our houseguest finds him interesting enough to ride all the way to town, hide her mount behind the haberdashery, and sneak into the churchyard just to see him go about his morning ritual of practicing a sermon."

"You are wrong on both assumptions, my lord. I had no desire to spy on Mr. Fernley, and I do not like spiders."

"Then you must have some other reason for being here so early in the morning. Is there something I can help you with?"

He knew why she was sneaking around, and the half smile on his face told her he wasn't amused. Her decision to form an alliance and stop vexing the man ended with the realization that he had known she was following him. "You are a wicked man."

Lord Grafton raised his eyebrows as he narrowed his eyes. "What constitutes the qualities of a wicked man?"

Briar's eyes went wide. The audacity of his question rendered her speechless.

"Very well, Miss Kensington. I will allow you to think upon your answer. But I have one more question for you. You followed me into town for a purpose. What can I do for you?"

She scrambled for any excuse that would sound legitimate, but then remembered her purpose in going to town hadn't been to follow him. She'd given up the search. She'd come for an entirely different reason. "If you must know, I came to meditate and pray."

"Such spiritual matters are generally done inside the church house."

She was annoyed by his ability to dissect everything she said and find fault. It was all very confusing, and as she looked into his eyes and got lost in the deep blue similarities to the most beautiful parts of the ocean, she found herself at a loss for words. Her voice wouldn't work, but had she formulated a response worth sharing? Had her brain communicated to her mouth? Everything was blank, and when he kept looking at her like he expected an answer, one she couldn't give, because it was far too complicated to share, she decided she had to say something. Gathering her courage, she brazenly asked, "What brought you to town so early in the morning?"

"The vicarage falls under the responsibility of my estate. I came into town to make certain the workers arrived to replace the roof. It started leaking two days ago, and the damage will only increase as it continues to snow."

Gathering her wits, Briar smugly smiled. "I suppose it was too much of an assumption to believe you are a praying man."

He didn't respond with words. Instead, his face had the same tortured confused smile he'd worn when first visiting Kensington Park. What did that expression mean? Was it his way of telling those around him he was merely there to perform his duty? She wasn't certain finding out the entirety of his facial expression was necessary. An overwhelming sense of shame entered her chest and heat rose from her neck and landed in her cheeks.

Briar knew she'd been impertinent. His responses left her even more vulnerable than his eyes. Remembering her purpose in following him, Briar made her confession. "I intended to find you this morning, my lord. I wanted to apologize for my assumptions yesterday. It was inappropriate for me to question your judgement on the ruins and your position as magistrate. And now my unfounded accusations regarding your spiritual dedication were cruel. I have been a very ungrateful guest, and I intend to do better."

"Thank you for saying as much. I have not made your time in Yorkshire easy, and I apologize. I should never have been so unbending upon our first meeting. I hope you will find it within yourself to forgive me."

She hadn't expected such a heartfelt apology. The words momentarily took her by surprise. She saw a soft sincerity in his eyes and his jaw was slack, and if she was correct, he was smiling at her. It wasn't a full joyful smile, but she found it more pleasing than a tooth-bearing grin. Briar didn't know what was happening to her desire to vex him, but suddenly she wanted nothing more than to spend an evening in quiet conversation with Earl Grafton.

"Will you allow me to escort you back to Primrose Hall?"

"Yes." She would have agreed to anything with the softness of his speech and the kindness in his eyes. Her normal thoughts of his odious and wicked behavior were lost as she looked upon his pleasing countenance. Shaking her mind free of the fanciful thoughts forcing their way to the surface, she found her way back to reality.

She would have to meditate in her chambers, for she couldn't deny the earl after they'd formed an understanding of sorts. Giving a nod of agreement, Briar stepped away from the window onto the footpath that would take her back to her horse. Instead of a graceful walk, she slipped in the mud, one foot sliding forward while the other stayed rooted where it was. To her astonishment, Lord Grafton's arms took hold of her, assisting her to regain balance. "Thank you, my lord. I believe you saved me a mess of bruises."

"You are most welcome. Take care where you step; it would not be good for you to slip twice in one morning." Lord Grafton kept hold of her arm until she was safely back on her horse.

She waited until he was riding next to her to ask about his horse. She hoped he would not be bothered by her question. "My lord, is there a meaning behind the name you have given your mount? Sugar Plum seems an unusual name for a horse."

Lord Grafton's jaw visibly clenched and then softened. "Yes. When I was younger, one of my siblings and I would sneak into the kitchens on Twelfth Night and eat sugar plums to our heart's content."

Briar could easily imagine a young Lord Grafton, sneaking into the pantry with Archie when the cook and maids were busy in other areas of the house. "Let me guess, you and Archie?"

A genuine laugh escaped with a mischievous glint of pleasure. "Archie would have ruined the entire escapade by tripping over his feet and falling down the stairs. We would have been discovered long before we found the treats."

"Phineas then. I cannot believe Gilbert would behave like a scamp."

"Neither of them."

"Oliver would have been too young. And Cornelius does not look to be a scalawag. Fletcher would have chatted the entire time, so I cannot imagine you would have dragged him along." Briar turned her head to the side so she could see past the sides of her bonnet. "Which sibling did you convince to steal sugar plums with you?"

Lord Grafton's smile turned from pleasure to nostalgia. She knew too well the way a person's face looked when remembering and longing for a repeat of time long in the past. Her heart went out to him. "I had a sister. Her name was Esther. She was vibrant and full of life. She could walk without a sound down the most antiquated staircase to cause mischief or to loot an unsuspecting pantry."

Affection filled his entire body, and Briar was certain she was witnessing a genuine side of Lord Grafton. The odious earl was replaced with a devoted family man. He sat astride his horse with posture to rival the King of England, sharing vulnerable memories of a sister long gone.

Briar shouldn't have found him dashing. She didn't want to admire him. But as she watched the memories dance across his face with laughter and smiles of long-ago childhood antics, a pang of longing entered her chest with a heaviness she hadn't expected. He understood grief. She envied his ability to speak freely about his sister and hoped one day to have the same control of her emotions. One day she would be able to speak of her parents without tears.

As they rode back to Primrose Hall, Briar silently fought her growing attraction to Lord Grafton. He was a true gentleman. Even his stiff posture didn't bother her as she thought about his generosity toward others. Her mind drifted to the suitability of a match with him. Before she allowed her thoughts to indulge in the obvious admiration she felt, she stopped herself. The gentle, kind man sitting atop his horse would never accept a wife who hadn't been bred for the role of a countess. Even her grandfather hadn't considered Lord Grafton as a match. He'd clearly stated she should consider the Fernley men. Not the earl. Therefore, it was best she not form an attachment because it would only end in disappointment.

Chapter Sixteen

Although it seemed like the sun would never shine again and his life would never be whole due to the loss of his father, Baxter somehow found hope budding like the first signs of spring within his soul. He couldn't pinpoint the reason for this newfound desire for life, but it was a wonderful feeling to get out of bed each morning knowing there was more to do than run an estate.

He fully realized he'd spent every moment of the last year dreading each day due to a self-imposed need to perfect his position amongst the gentry. But the desire for perfection melted away as the earth around him stayed in a frozen wintery state. Even the cold didn't take the newfound cheerfulness away.

Baxter hummed as he entered the morning room, but abruptly stopped as he heard Mr. Hayes's high-pitched giggle. He tried not to let his disappointment show as his desire to be with people dissipated. He'd hoped for a morning without visitors. A time he could spend with his family and Miss Kensington. But Mr. Hayes had started visiting each morning, and it seemed like he was always there.

He would need to speak with Hayes. If the man wanted a courtship, it was inappropriate for the visits to continue without

ANGELA JOHNSON

making it official. Propriety dictated he request permission from Miss Kensington's guardian. As Baxter sat across the room, listening to the peacock in bright blue pantaloons and a sunflower yellow waistcoat dazzle Miss Kensington, he wondered why he was torturing himself by sitting in the room enduring the ridiculous conversation.

His last interaction with Miss Kensington had left him invigorated and hopeful for more. He'd given up the internal argument against forming an attachment. Now he needed to decide on a plan of action. Most men in his position would speak with the young lady's guardian and arrange a marriage before another man could steal her away, but something within him told him that was not the way to win Miss Kensington's admiration. She needed to be wooed, and he would do everything in his power to declare his intentions. He would do so when Hayes was not around, with his overexaggerated mannerisms and ridiculous behavior.

Choosing sanity over Mr. Hayes's latest gossip, Baxter assigned Archibald to oversee the visit and he left the house in search of solitude. There was much to consider regarding his family and the possibility of courting Miss Kensington.

Phineas would leave for Egypt as soon as the snow melted. Archie planned to spend his summer months at the estate in Scotland writing. Fletcher would return to London and resume his life as a barrister before long, and no one knew when Cornelius would be called back to duty as there was always a war to fight somewhere. He was thankful Gilbert would be close by. As the local vicar, this brother would always be near Primrose Hall. The last of his brothers was Oliver, a levelheaded musician who had no way of providing a living for himself outside of teaching music. Each one needed his help, and Baxter had to figure out how to lend his assistance without it being obvious.

With the connections his father had passed onto him, there was much Baxter could do to guide his brothers. Needing advice, Baxter rode his horse to the churchyard cemetery to discuss his thoughts with his father. Entering through the kissing gate, he walked past an ancient willow tree as the snow crunched under his weight. As he neared his destination, he kissed his fingers and placed them on his twin sister's headstone. But he wasn't there to visit with Esther. Baxter stepped past two more headstones to stand before his father's final resting place. Wiping the snow from the headstone, Baxter knelt upon the snow, threw his hat on the top of the marker bearing the name William Fernley, the fifth Earl of Grafton, and spoke his thoughts.

"I am certain it comes as no surprise to you that Phineas wants to go to Egypt. I am worried about him. I cannot persuade him to stay, and so I have given him my blessing. But I regret my decision to do so, and I do not know how to keep him safe. Is it wrong of me to want to hold him back?"

Baxter stopped speaking at the sound of horse hooves and carriage wheels. He stood and turned around as he saw a footman assisting Gigi. He knew she visited the cemetery, but it was usually on Sunday mornings before services.

It didn't take her long to follow the same path he'd walked only moments before. "I thought I would find you out here." His mother handed him a wreath, and Baxter placed it next to the headstone.

"Did Mr. Hayes depart Primrose Hall?" Baxter needed to know that Miss Kensington wasn't left unchaperoned.

"Yes, he and Archie chose to go for a ride, and Miss Kensington decided to stay behind."

Baxter kept his relief inward. He didn't want Gigi suspecting the internal struggle he fought over Miss Kensington. He wanted to explore the feelings on his own and possibly speak to his father's headstone over the situation.

"You have had much weighing on you this last year."

He chuckled as he ran a hand through his hair. "I did not think anyone had noticed."

"How could I not? You have been distant, and I am concerned

over you locking yourself away in the library and den. I fear you will catch your death with the time you spend at the ruins, especially when it is snowing. Speak to me, Baxter. I can lend advice where your father cannot."

"I will join the family more often, if you wish."

Gigi didn't relent. "What has you so distracted?"

"My brothers." With this one small confession, Baxter unloaded all his familial concerns onto his mother. She didn't need the extra burden, but he yearned for her advice.

"Baxter, it is admirable of you to be so concerned, but none of this is new information. Your father and I discussed each of these problems and decided to allow each of you boys to find your way in the world."

"Are you telling me I should not worry over Phineas leaving the country? What if he arrives in Egypt and travels to the Valley of the Kings and falls into a pit? How would we know of his fate?"

"His decision has not been made lightly. Phineas is aware of the consequences of leaving England."

"I do not like it."

"It is not within your control. Your time would be better spent focusing on your duties."

Baxter couldn't push his concerns aside so easily. "What about Cornelius? He could end up in a skirmish far worse than he has experienced thus far. When he leaves this next time for France or some other awful war, it could be the last time we see him alive."

"When Cornelius left for the Iberian Peninsula, your father and I realized we could not stop our sons from their dreams. We purchased a commission for Cornelius in hopes of keeping him out of the worst parts of war. If we couldn't convince Cornelius from his course of action, you will have no power to stop your brothers from their interests and pursuits."

"As earl, it is my duty to see each of my brothers succeed in their endeavors. I cannot sit back and enjoy the fruits of my inheritance while they struggle. I have been gifted an entire estate with more than I need. Why is it so difficult for them to accept my assistance."

"It is very admirable of you to think this way, but you are wrong. You are forgetting the most important part of your duty is to find a wife and produce an heir. Have you even thought about this?"

Baxter sheepishly looked away from his mother. He didn't want her to see the truth of his intentions for Miss Kensington, not yet. "How can I focus on myself when the family is falling apart? If everyone leaves, there will be nothing left of Primrose Hall."

"They have to leave. Your uncles and aunts did not stay here once your father and I married. They each found their way in life, and a new generation of Fernley's thrived upon the estate. Now it is time for your brothers to move away. They will come back for visits, and over time, you and your future wife will raise a family, and when your heir takes his place, his siblings will leave as well."

"I do not want to lose my brothers. I cannot lose them. They are my friends and confidants. I have spent my entire life with all of them. How can I let them go?"

"Do not be silly. There is no reason for this exaggerated attachment. I do not know what has come over you."

Baxter knew exactly what it was. Loss was too prevalent in their lives. He well remembered his twin sister losing her battle to live when they were children, and the recent loss of his father had dredged up those feelings and added a new deepening sense of loss. It had affected him more than he'd expected. The thought of losing one more family member to illness, and seeing another casket lowered into the ground, was too much for him to bear. Looking into Gigi's concerned eyes, Baxter couldn't burden her with his thoughts, but he could make his mother a promise. He would not shirk his duty. "I will do my best to find a wife and provide an heir."

"Good. I hoped you would say as much."

Her excitement left him curious but hesitant. "Do you have a woman in mind?"

Gigi's eyes lit up with pleasure. "I am so glad you asked. Briar is my choice."

Baxter raised his eyebrows in surprise. He would admit nothing to his mother. It wasn't proper as he was her protector. He also hadn't done anything to show his intentions toward Miss Kensington.

"She and I have an understanding that I consider her my daughter, and she has allowed me to fill the role of surrogate mother. I only need you to make it official by offering for her hand."

"Miss Kensington despises me. I fear her heart will never soften." This was one of his many reasons for holding back. He would not use his position and title to force a woman into admiration. If she could never love him, then he would do his best to move past the longing he had for her.

"She will soften, over time. You must show her who you truly are. She only knows the unbending earl who made a disastrous first impression."

He could not deny his foolish words had caused the formation of an enemy. "I will think about it and consider my options, but only after I have resolved my distress over my brothers."

"Oh, dear." Gigi shook her head in disappointment. "Can you not see the burden on your shoulders has nothing to do with your brothers, but everything to do with the feelings you are suppressing for Briar? You were not so distressed until you met her."

Offended by the assumption, Baxter took a step back. What did Gigi know of his feelings for Miss Kensington? Had he been so obvious? "I was concerned about my family before her arrival."

"Until you open your eyes and realize how you feel, I fear you will never get rid of this heavy burden you carry."

"You cannot manipulate me into thinking I feel anything except contempt for Miss Kensington." He didn't know why he was saying such things. He no longer felt that way about her. He was confused and needed time to formulate a plan of action for the sake of propriety. It was quite possible he would have to wait until her grandfather returned from France to court the stubborn, sassy, yet thoroughly encaptivating Miss Kensington.

"I have no intention of manipulating you or the circumstances. But I would appreciate it if you would make an effort to be kind. All this arguing you do with Briar will never allow you to be open and show your true self to the young lady. She cannot fall in love with such a stuffy man."

"Stuffy?" Baxter had never been treated so abominably by his mother. "What have I done to deserve your censure?"

"You bored the life out of Briar while showing her the house."

Baxter put his hands on his hips. "I was attempting to inform her about the history of Primrose Hall."

"By describing the plaster?"

Baxter let his hands fall to the side, no longer in a defensive stance. "You heard about that?"

"Of course I did. The maids overheard the tour and have spoken of nothing else since."

Baxter knew the heat around his neck wasn't from his winter clothing. It wouldn't be long before his face was bright red in embarrassment. "I suppose I could have made more of an effort."

Gigi reached out and put her hands on the sides of his face. She pulled his head toward her, so he was bending but at her eye level. "You have changed since your father's death. I understand the burden you carry, but you cannot let it take the best parts of who you are away from us. Please, find the man I know you to be and bring him back to Primrose Hall."

Baxter allowed his mother to kiss him on the forehead, and then he walked her back to the carriage and assisted her to her seat. He had much to think about. Instead of going back to the warmth of his home, he mounted his horse and rode up to the ruins. He didn't know how to bring his old self back. Had he changed so much over the last year that the parts of him that found joy in life were gone?

Was he now an ornery earl who only cared about duty? If he couldn't be the kind and generous man he once was, what would he do about his growing admiration for Briar Kensington? She deserved better than he'd given her, Gigi was right on that observation.

As Baxter carefully climbed up the ice ridden steps to sit on the stone wall overlooking his land, he wondered how he could show his true self to Miss Kensington. She was beautiful, and her blush set his heart pounding. He loved hearing the chime of her laugh, and he found her excitement about the ruins intoxicating. He had no idea how to bridge the gap that lay between them. She had every right to despise him—he'd given her nothing to like about him or his country. Yet, their last encounter at the churchyard and her listening ear had given him a small amount of hope. They'd formed an understanding, which he could now use to his advantage and possibly let her see his true self.

Shivering from the cold air, Baxter entered the drawing room looking for tea and a warm fire, but he found it full of women from the surrounding area. "Ames, I will take my tea in the library."

"No, you will not." Gigi crossed the room and took his arm. "Your brothers were supposed to help us with these charity baskets, but I have not seen any of them since this morning." Gigi gave Ames a pointed look. He knew the butler understood the command. Tea would be brought into the drawing room.

It would be futile to argue with Gigi, so Baxter allowed her to pull him across the room, where she forced him into one of the armchairs, next to Miss Kensington. He'd made the decision to show her his charms, and so without delay and offering no argument, he went to work stuffing the baskets with usable items.

When he'd been a lad, his mother had taught him the finer points of serving those less fortunate. He knew how to build a charity basket, and he hoped to impress Miss Kensington with his skills.

"Miss Kensington, did you and your neighbors gather in Boston to make charity baskets?"

"We did, quite often."

"What sorts of offerings would you give?"

"Breads, pies, and little candies. Much the same as what is in these. We would also arrange baskets with medical supplies when necessary."

Baxter picked up a blue hair ribbon and held it out. "Would you include such important items as ribbons?"

"Very much so, my lord. A girl of any circumstance must have hair ribbons."

Baxter enjoyed seeing Miss Kensington's smile. Her cheeks were rosy, but not from embarrassment. She was smiling out of pleasure, which left him breathless. As he made little comments that seemed trite, she opened, and a sparkle of amusement entered her eyes. Baxter was certain he'd never had such enjoyment while putting together charity baskets.

He marveled over the seemingly small effort he'd made. If that was all it would take to win the woman over, he would have her swooning in his arms before supper. Baxter spent the entire day with Gigi and Miss Kensington in the sleigh, delivering gifts. He didn't spare a thought for all the work left undone on his desk nor the hours it would take away from his rest to check the ledgers. Instead, he enjoyed the afternoon and put all his worries aside.

Chapter Seventeen

Evenings at Primrose Hall had become Briar's favorite part of the day. She enjoyed the quiet conversations, the winding down from a busy day, and the ability to learn about each of the Fernley men. As she sat next to Oliver, he pulled out a thin rectangular box and handed it to her. "I hope you do not find me presumptuous, but I thought you would enjoy this."

Briar blushed. It wasn't proper to accept gifts from a man she wasn't engaged to, but since Oliver was more like a brother, could she justify a little gift? "What is it?" She took the box, unable to hold back a smile as she unclasped the lock and lifted the top. "A flute?"

"Yes, I thought you would want to learn how to play."

Looking over the beautiful instrument, she ran her hand along the shiny silver, touching every inch of it. The cold metal brought tears to her eyes. Briar knew she couldn't accept it. She'd wanted to learn the flute, especially after hearing Oliver's masterful way with the instrument, but it wasn't right. She closed the lid and held it out so Oliver could take it back. "It is too much."

Oliver shook his head and pushed the box toward her. "I wanted to get this for you. I can teach you how to play, and we can perform a duet."

"But it is inappropriate for me to accept such an expensive gift."

Oliver rolled his eyes and shook his head. "Briar, it is only inappropriate if you let it be. My reason for giving this to you is purely selfish. I need to practice teaching a novice at the flute."

"Why?" She knew he had little from his father's estate. Being the youngest son, it was barely enough for him to live on. He would need to find a woman with a dowry or a wealthy heiress to pad his personal coffers. "Whom do you plan to teach after me?"

"Once I am proficient at instruction on the flute, I can seek students, and I can be free from the burden of poverty."

Briar knew there were specific professions the *ton* deemed suitable. She was certain a music instructor was not one of them. "Will Lord Grafton allow you to take a profession such as school master?"

"Baxter does not get to choose my path. I have to make those decisions."

Briar nodded in agreement. She did think the earl overstepped, especially with Phineas. "I think it is admirable to want to teach others how to use instruments as you do."

"Then you will allow me to instruct you?"

His hopeful eyes left her wondering how she could deny him. She worried another argument would burst out during supper when Lord Grafton discovered the gift, but she agreed with Oliver—he needed to find a way to support himself. "I will agree this one time, but please do not purchase anything else for me. It is inappropriate."

Oliver leaned toward her and whispered. "Not if we were engaged."

She'd already decided Oliver was not the right man for her, so she hoped he was teasing. He had to see how ill fitted they were. "Do not jest with me, Oliver. You know we are ill-suited."

"Why? What is it about me that you do not like?"

Briar realized he was in earnest as his head turned down and he refused to look at her. She had to be delicate. "I admire everything about you. But I love you as I would a brother. I cannot see any other future before us."

"Is it because of Mr. Hayes? I can dress as ridiculously as he does and bore everyone with topics of little consequences, if that is the sort of man you want."

Briar shook her head with vigor. Another talkative man was far from what she desired. "I want you to stay exactly as you are now. You have a wonderful sense of humor, and you are kind. One day, you will meet a woman who fits with your personality, but I am afraid I am too serious."

Briar knew she couldn't accept the gift, not now that she had broken Oliver's heart. "Save this for when you find the right woman."

He cleared his throat, and with a shaky laugh, he pushed the flute back to her. "You must allow me to instruct you now. Otherwise, you will have destroyed both my heart and my hopes for future employment all in one evening."

"I have not injured you too much. You still want to be my friend?"

Oliver's smile didn't reach his eyes. "I want to be the brother you imagine. Friends cannot give each other gifts like this, but brothers are allowed."

"Oliver, I do not know what to say."

"Agree to my instruction and promise to forget my foolish behavior."

Briar hoped they would find a comfortable friendship again, and so she agreed. She followed his instructions on how to sit with a posture that would allow her to breathe while using the instrument, and then she listened as he explained how to place her fingers over each hole. She tried to ignore the aching in her heart as his somber expression reached his eyes.

Momentarily, she wondered if it was possible to take what she had said back. She could pretend to feel more than sisterly affection for him. A life with Oliver wouldn't be terrible. But she knew it would be wrong to deceive him. She focused on the instrument instead of his jittery hands. She would do everything she could to recommend him to another woman when next he decided to find love.

BRIAR DIDN'T KNOW WHAT TO THINK ABOUT MR. HAYES'S continued visits. After weeks of seeing him every morning, his bright clothing and conversation were wearing on her nerves. But more than Mr. Hayes's visits, the continued wistfulness in Oliver's eyes when he looked toward her left Briar unsettled. Courtship and love should be a time of cheerful bliss, but she didn't find such feelings with either Mr. Hayes or Oliver.

When Mr. Hayes offered to take her for a ride, she hoped it would be to the ruins as he'd promised, but Hayes directed the horses in the opposite direction, so she sat back and admired the countryside.

Mr. Hayes had the ability to speak about everything and nothing at the same time. His word definitions and little-known facts about Society, India, Africa, and America, were enough to make her fall asleep, but she had to admit he was kind, and kindness was a rare quality.

Mr. Hayes, in a pair of bright green pantaloons and a purple waistcoat, dominated the conversation as usual. "Did you know that only a third of the American Colonists actually supported the war for independence? It is said most of the Colonists switched sides depending on who they thought was winning."

Briar nodded as she usually did to let him think she was listening. Instead of focusing on the conversation, Briar thought about the displeasure on Lord Grafton's face that morning. It was no wonder Lord Grafton continued to despise her. Every time he entered a room, he had to hear facts about the states from Mr. Hayes. Had she made Hayes think she wanted to hear his facts about the colonies? Even she was sick of listening to the history of her country from this man.

"Mr. Hayes," Briar said, interrupting his discussion on what George Washington must have felt while leading a new country.

"I have often wondered if Mr. Washington realized he would have to"—Hayes stopped speaking as he realized she'd said his name —"Yes?"

"Do you ever take time to sit and ponder over the beauty of this country you live in?"

Hayes's mouth turned down in concentration. "Whatever do you mean?"

"I wish I could ride my horse to the top of a hill and overlook a valley filled with trees and lakes and simply enjoy a moment of silence, reflecting on all of the wonders and creations of God. Have you ever thought about doing that?"

Mr. Hayes looked at her with confusion. "No. I admit I have never had the desire. Why ever would you want to be alone? Conversation is much more pleasing."

"Oh."

"Now, back to what I was saying about Mr. Washington."

Briar stopped listening to him. He didn't need her to respond, and she knew he wasn't expecting any comments from her. She passed the entire ride wishing it was already over. He was a kind man, but she didn't know if she could handle marrying someone who talked as much as he did and brushed aside the desires of her heart.

It was the second strike against him. She didn't like his sense of fashion, and she had grown weary of his constant talking. The only positive thing she could think of, regarding his continued attempts at courting, was that he was making an effort. No one else in all of Yorkshire, even Oliver, had asked to take her on a carriage ride or come to visit her each day. She was living in a house full of men, and only one of them had shown interest in her. She knew Oliver wasn't right for her just as she feared Mr. Hayes wasn't a match. Her situation seemed hopeless. She couldn't continue to be a burden upon Lord Grafton and his family, and she didn't know when her grandfather would return, but could she continue courting a man she didn't care for?

As Briar dressed for a musical evening, she found her heart wasn't prepared for an evening of guests. She preferred spending her evenings with Gigi and the Fernley brothers in the drawing room. Each one of the men would be lifetime friends, apart from Lord Grafton. She had hoped they'd made progress, but she didn't know if it would be possible to ever consider him a friend.

In the evenings, Lord Grafton was quiet and spent most of his time in a chair near the window with a book or a newspaper. He wasn't much of a conversationalist, which intrigued her. He watched as Oliver taught her the flute, and she wondered what he thought of the entire situation. Since he never mentioned it, she assumed he didn't mind, but she did fear he would assume a courtship since Oliver had gifted her an instrument.

With her hair pulled up in an elegant coiffeur, wearing a cream muslin gown sprinkled with embroidered blue flowers, Briar knew she would spend the evening wishing for a heavier material on her dress. Even the wrap she had around her shoulders wouldn't suffice for the cold night. She was ready for spring and had decided the warmth of the sun couldn't come fast enough.

As she descended the stairs, Briar mentally prepared herself for Mr. Hayes and his never-ending list of facts. She inwardly chided herself for not being more excited over Mr. Hayes. He was a good man, even if he did love the sound of his own voice.

"Miss Kensington, you look ready to dazzle us with talent this evening." Mr. Hayes's comment made her smile but only out of a sense of duty. She noted the lack of heat in her cheeks and realized she was far too used to his compliments to feel any pleasure over them. "Please tell me you have prepared a song for us."

"Mr. Fernley and I have practiced together. If Oliver is willing to accompany me, I will be happy to sing," She looked to Oliver to confirm his part in her performance. She could sing perfectly, when accompanied by the piano. She always lost her nerve when required to sing without music and ended up off-key and embarrassed.

She knew Oliver had harbored hopes of performing a duet with her on the flute, but she wasn't ready to share those talents with others. She could perform short nursery songs, but none of them were grand enough for a party.

"I would be happy to assist." Oliver bowed his head in acceptance. For a moment, she found a yearning within and she wished Oliver was the man who would make her happy. They had shared interests and he was entertaining and attentive, but she knew happiness with him would wane over time.

Looping her arm through Mr. Hayes's, Briar followed him into the drawing room, which had been set up for the musical soiree. Primrose Hall was filled with the same people as the last party, and Briar hoped she would remember most of their names.

As her mind was focused on making a match, Briar found Captain Cornelius Fernley dressed in his uniform sitting by himself in a corner of the room. He wasn't a contemplative man. Extracting her arm from Mr. Hayes, she excused herself. When he didn't acknowledge her departure, Briar bit her bottom lip to push back the pain of being ignored. Mr. Hayes was in his element. He had an audience ready to listen to his stories, and she was only hindering his socializing.

Briar moved toward the corner of the room, hoping to converse with Mr. Cornelius Fernley. Although she was on first names with most of the Fernley men, Cornelius and Lord Grafton were the two with whom she hadn't formed a comfortable attachment.

"Mr. Fernley, do you mind if I sit with you for a moment?"

Cornelius stood and motioned toward the chair adjacent to his. She was thankful he hadn't turned her away even though she knew by his secluded spot in the room that he didn't want the company.

"Do you not enjoy parties?" Briar asked.

Cornelius gave a brief smile but went back to looking out the window. "It depends on who is in attendance."

"Do you not have anyone here you care to socialize with? Surely you know everyone."

"The conversations I will have with these people now will not mean anything when I see them again. I will be leaving for France before the end of the month."

Briar sat in silence, not knowing what to say. She hadn't heard anything about his upcoming departure. "Your family has behaved as though everyone will be here until summer. Why has no one mentioned your leaving?"

Cornelius sat back in his chair and finally turned his gaze upon her. "Gigi and Baxter are unaware. I ask you to not speak of it until I have a chance to inform them."

"But why would you not tell your mother and brother?" She didn't want to be in possession of such a secret. She could keep it, but such valuable information was not supposed to be kept silent. "They would want to know of your plans."

Cornelius chuckled and tapped his fingers on his leg. "Gigi will cry and sequester herself in her chambers while she comes to terms with my leaving, which will mean I will have less time to spend with her. Baxter will send a letter to headquarters in London requesting I have more time with my family in Yorkshire. I have been here since my father's death, and Baxter refuses to let me leave. My other brothers are all aware I am leaving, but they have agreed to keep silent on the topic until I am ready to share with Gigi and Baxter."

"I think you are noble and brave, Mr. Fernley, and it is important to defend your way of life and your country. You have my word. I will stay silent on this information."

"You must call me Cornelius. I cannot continue being the only one you refer to so formally."

"I agree. And you may use my Christian name as well." Since she knew Cornelius was leaving Yorkshire, it meant he was likely not looking for marriage. Therefore, his name was promptly eliminated from her list of possible suitors.

Surveying the rest of the room, she noticed one person was missing. Lord Grafton had yet to make an appearance. Was he planning to spend his evening alone? Briar was convinced if she had to attend the musical and sing for these strangers, Lord Grafton should have to attend as well. She needed to forget his past wrongs and truly offer the hand of friendship. Excusing herself, she left the drawing room and made her way to the library. She'd never been inside the room as she was fully aware it was Lord Grafton's domain, but a part of her ached to know he would be sitting alone, and she wouldn't allow it.

Candlelight streamed out the partially open door, and she could see Lord Grafton standing near the window, his back to the room. Briar took a deep breath to gather courage before rapping lightly on the door. As he turned around, she saw his surprise at her presence, but there was also an unreadable expression on his face. Was he happy to see her? Did he want to compliment her? Or was he trying to find a nice way to send her back to the drawing room? She found her legs a bit wobbly, but she pressed forward.

"Miss Kensington, is something wrong?"

"No, my lord, I noticed you had not joined the party, and I decided if you could escape the night's events, so could I." In a brazen move, Briar crossed the room and sat in a chair near the fire.

Sitting so close to the flames took all her concerns for a cold evening away.

Surprising Briar, Lord Grafton walked to the chair across from her and sat. He crossed one leg over the other. She noted he was dressed for the party, so he must have been planning to attend.

"Where are your admirers?"

Briar blushed. She knew who he was speaking of. "Mr. Hayes is currently occupied with a retelling of his latest discovery on muslin."

"Muslin?" Grafton's confused expression put a smile on her face.

"Yes. He discovered a shipment of fine muslin that no one had claimed. He is now an investor and will sell the goods to local merchants."

"Is there anything of interest in the retelling of this story?"

Briar shook her head. "No. But he is willing to share all details if you are interested."

"I am not."

She sat further back on the chair finding it a very comfortable spot. The library was more than she'd expected. Looking at the walls of books, she wanted to search through everything to know what options there were for reading. "You have a beautiful library. It is no wonder you spend so much time in here."

"You are welcome to borrow any of the books. I have a ledger by the door to record any book that is removed from the room. I only ask you make certain to return whatever you take when finished."

"Thank you. I will accept that offer." She stood and walked to the closest shelf so she could see the titles. As the gentleman he was, Lord Grafton also stood. "Do you have a favorite?"

"I have not read anything enjoyable for quite some time."

"Then what do you do while you are in here?"

"I am currently studying books on estate management. It is a dull topic, but one I must understand."

Briar turned to look at him. "Do you not enjoy commanding an entire estate?"

"I am very proud to be the one entrusted with the legacy of the title." Lord Grafton puffed his chest out a little, correcting any lax in posture. "I was born to the duty, and I take it seriously."

"I have noticed."

"What do you mean?"

Briar walked back to her seat and made herself comfortable. "Please do not misunderstand what I am saying. I admire your convictions and the way you maintain this beautiful house and the land, but I wonder if you find any joy in your duty."

She could see he was holding back to not lose his temper, and she was thankful. If they could have a civil conversation without jumping to conclusions, with a great deal of effort, they might even be able to build a friendship.

"You are right, Miss Kensington. I do not find joy in my circumstances."

"Why?"

Lord Grafton retook his seat and sat with his hands steepled against his chin in a ponderous pose. "I do not like change, but no matter what I do, my father is still gone, my brothers will leave by spring, and I will be left here trying to keep everything frozen with the memory of my family and what life was like just over a year ago."

It was another vulnerable answer, and she was shocked to find he had shared a bit more of his soul with her. Who was the man sitting across from her? It certainly wasn't the Lord Grafton who'd accused her of improper behavior and personally forcing the king to insanity. This was a return to the gentleman who'd ridden next to her across a frozen field while speaking of a long dead sister.

Lord Grafton met her eyes, daring her to give him an answer. She wanted to solve all his problems and say something brilliant, but the only words to enter her mind seemed insufficient. "Although your world seems to have stopped with the late earl's death, you are still here, and you must find a way to make him proud. Your title and position in Society give you the ability to make a difference in the world, so stop sitting in this dark library and find a way to make your father's legacy count."

"You are very wise, Miss Kensington."

Briar gave a little nod of thanks and continued prodding. "What is the one thing you have to do right now to ensure the legacy your father left will survive?"

Lord Grafton's eyes went wide, and she wondered what was happening in his mind. Was his brain going through all the duties he was to perform to find the most important, or did he already know what it was, and he didn't want to say it out loud? She wasn't going to give him any hints or help him unless he contributed to the conversation, and so she waited for an answer.

Lord Grafton adjusted in his seat and looked into her eyes, leaving her stunned by the intensity. "I must find a wife and produce an heir. That is the most important duty I have to my family and title."

She knew the British were determined to bring sons into the aristocracy because wealth and land were passed to the eldest living male. Daughters were not as useful unless it was to form an alliance with a wealthier or well-connected family. She was thankfully not worried about such things. As her grandfather's heiress, she knew there would be men who wanted her dowry and the financial freedom her money would offer, but she wanted love, and she wondered what Lord Grafton wanted outside of an heir.

She could help him in his search. "What attributes are you looking for in a wife?"

Lord Grafton's expression changed back to that unreadable pained smile she'd seen two other times, and she wondered what it meant. "I have not given it much thought."

"I am certain you could find a willing woman tonight, if you made an effort."

Lord Grafton's face stayed plastered in that indiscernible expression that made him look like he was suffering an apoplexy. She didn't like it. "I have never had to make an effort, Miss Kensington."

She wasn't certain if he was teasing her, but a hint of a smile peeked through the austere earl persona she disliked so much. "Whatever do you mean? I do not see any evidence of women standing in line waiting for you to offer marriage."

"Then you have not paid enough attention at these parties. I am an earl, and I am wealthy. Those are the only attributes a mother with unmarried daughters needs to make a match amongst the *ton*."

"Then you could marry and fulfill one part of your duty before the summer. Why do you delay?"

His lips twisted, and he looked away from her. Briar wondered if she had said something wrong. She knew marriage in his position wasn't done without expectations on both sides for furthering their position in Society.

"I do not know."

Unable to stop her sassy comment because she loved vexing the man, she tried to say it with a smile to make him laugh. Unfortunately, it had the opposite effect. "I thought you were the kind of man to never shirk his duty."

She saw a flash of irritation in his eyes, but he didn't argue. Instead, he stood and offered her his arm. "It is best we join our guests. The musical will start soon, and I am told you plan to perform with Oliver."

Briar knew she'd been far too bold with the rebuke she'd given, but she wasn't repentant of her words until she took notice of the women flocking to his side. Lord Grafton was never without a debutante and an eager mother monopolizing his evening. She needed to apologize, but her pride wouldn't allow it. She had only one man seeking her attention, and he was grating on her nerves. The women vying for Lord Grafton's attention didn't speak endlessly about absolutely nothing, and they had a good fashion sense. She decided, he had nothing to complain about.

Chapter Eighteen

"She is brazen and insolent!" Baxter said, as he paced through the library. "How dare she give me advice on how to handle myself with my title?" He looked to Gigi expecting her to agree; instead she glowed, and her eyes were cheerful.

"Often times, I find offense when someone speaks the words I need to hear. What did she say to make you stomp around the room like a tyrant?"

"I am not stomping." Baxter stopped moving to prove he wasn't stomping, but it only made Gigi laugh at him. "All right, I was acting foolish."

"I am glad you noticed. Now, tell me what Briar said to send you into a fit."

Baxter moved to the sofa and sat next to Gigi. His legs were heavy aching for relief. "Miss Kensington gave me the wisdom and advice I would expect from father. How did she know what to say?"

"She is very wise, especially for her age."

"I am at a loss as to what to do."

Gigi took his hand and held it, much like she had when he was a

131

child. "It is never easy admitting when you have been a fool. I applaud you for noticing."

Baxter laughed as he laid his head on Gigi's shoulder. "Some real advice would be helpful."

"Stop secluding yourself and spend time with Briar. She is a beautiful woman, and if you do not find a way to make her your wife, I will disavow any knowledge of you as my son."

Baxter knew his mother was teasing with the latter part of her statement, but she was completely serious about a marriage. The only problem was he'd made Miss Kensington an enemy and had set the expectation for argument. "I have offended her so deeply. How can I ever make amends for my behavior?"

"Most people are very forgiving, when an apology is made."

"I do not think a simple *I am sorry* will suffice. I have already tried, and yet we continue to argue."

"I completely agree. Your efforts will need to go far beyond a trite statement." Gigi scooted forward on the sofa. "I trust you will work it out without my prying."

Baxter watched his mother leave. He buried his head in his hands hoping for a wave of inspiration on courting a woman he'd previously offended, but nothing came to him. When the clock on the mantle chimed the hour, he knew his daily tasks needed to take priority. So, he set out to meet with the steward. He usually found focusing on work could set his mind at ease.

As he stood in the yard, he noticed Miss Kensington riding away on her horse. A part of him wanted to ride after her and speak about anything other than their usual arguments, but he hadn't any idea what to say.

"My lord, do you want me to find another family to take on the responsibilities of the old Wilcox farm?"

Baxter looked to his steward and nodded. His mind was so preoccupied with Miss Kensington, he hadn't any idea what the man had asked, but he trusted him, and therefore there was no need to worry.

By the time everyone was gathered for supper, Baxter was still baffled about how to win over Miss Kensington. He hadn't any plan in place, so he quietly watched with envy, his ribs squeezing together, as Miss Kensington engaged in conversation with his brothers. He listened as they spoke of the musical from the night before, and his pulse quickened as Baxter realized he could join into the conversation. It wouldn't be so difficult to engage in small talk and little pleasantries. He prepared an observation and hoped at least one person would give a response.

With a lull in the conversation, Baxter placed his knife and fork on the table. "I was impressed with the violin recitation from Mr. and Miss Atkinson. I had no idea they were so talented."

To his utter astonishment, Miss Kensington was the first to respond. "It was the loveliest of all the performances. I have never heard two people harmonize so well. It was a joy to be in attendance."

Baxter appreciated her response. He smiled at Miss Kensington as his pulse quickened. He'd planned to praise Miss Kensington's performance next, but he stumbled over which word was most suitable.

Oliver, the youngest of his siblings and quite possibly the most annoying, interrupted any response Baxter could have formulated. "I believe Miss Atkinson has her cap set for you, Baxter. You should encourage her, and then we can have performances every night. I am certain her brother would regularly join us for supper, or I could step in if needed. I do play the violin quite well."

Baxter tried to sound unaffected, but his brother suggesting he court a different woman wouldn't help him woo Miss Kensington. "Thank you, Oliver. I was unaware of this."

"Even I am aware of Miss Atkinson's intentions," Miss Kensington said. She looked at Baxter with confusion. "Have you not noticed how she bats her eyes at you and laughs at everything you say? She stood by you for nearly an hour last night."

Baxter hadn't expected the conversation to change in this direction. He hadn't noticed Miss Atkinson. Did that make him aloof? "I admit, I did not. May I ask, why do women do that?"

"They are flirting with you, my lord." Miss Kensington's stunned and slow statement made Baxter feel stupid, yet it put his brothers into fits of laughter.

Baxter sat back in his chair reviewing the previous night. Miss Atkinson had stood at his side through most of his conversations talking about her new puppy, her excitement for the spring season in London, and a new pair of gloves she'd recently acquired, and she had giggled at everything he'd said. But her mother hadn't been nearby to convince him she was the perfect match. He was certain the only ones who wanted to marry him were dragged around by their mothers. Why hadn't Gigi pointed this out to him? How many other women did the same things as Miss Atkinson? This meant he had more admirers than he'd originally thought.

"Baxter, I fear you will never find a wife if you continue to ignore everyone and misunderstand their flirtatious clues." Archie wasn't trying to injure Baxter's feelings, and so he took the jest in stride.

Clearing his throat, Baxter had to put an end to the recommendation of Miss Atkinson. "I am afraid I cannot pursue her, even with her accomplishments on the violin."

"Why ever not?" Oliver shook his head in disgust. "She is handsome and would make a suitable wife for a man in your position."

"She is the daughter of a gentleman." Archie raised his eyebrows to show there was no reason to refuse the woman.

"A daughter of a gentleman has not been prepared for the duties of a countess. I must find a woman who can step into the role without hesitation." Baxter refused to look in Miss Kensington's direction for fear he had injured her. It was a great assumption on his part to think she harbored feelings of admiration, but if she did, his statement would be devastating.

"I disagree, Baxter." Gigi didn't have a problem looking between him and Miss Kensington. His throat constricted as she made her expectations obvious to anyone with eyes and a bit of sense. "Any woman can learn the duties of a countess with proper training."

Baxter nodded his head in deference to his mother. "I apologize, Gigi. If you wish me to court Miss Atkinson, I will do so with haste."

Gigi's eyes lit up with mischief. "I made my expectations clear when last we spoke. You know Miss Atkinson is not the woman I have encouraged you to marry."

"What?" Oliver grasped onto Fletcher and Cornelius who sat on either side of him. "Gigi has arranged a wife for you?"

Baxter expected nothing less from his youngest brother, who hadn't yet learned when discretion was necessary. Meeting his mother's mischievous grin, Baxter silently pleaded with her to keep their conversation private.

"Who is the fortunate woman? Does she know of her fate?" Oliver gazed around the room hoping someone would come to his aid and satisfy his curiosity. "Am I the only one in the family who does not yet know about the arrangement?"

Cornelius forcibly removed Oliver's clutched hand from his arm and dropped it without preamble. "With the scandalized expression upon Baxter's face, it is safe to assume he was recently informed."

Baxter lifted his serviette to his lips and lightly tapped to ensure he hadn't crumbs in the corners of his mouth. He kept his eyes locked upon Gigi in a silent battle of wills. He didn't know what she expected him to do in that moment. He wished he'd stayed out of the earlier conversation. As he finished wiping his mouth, Baxter replaced his serviette on his lap and quirked an eyebrow at his mother. "Would you like me to make an offer this evening? Or can we wait until I have had a chance to speak with the lady's guardian?"

"You may take your time. But please do so with haste. I would hate to think any of my sons were shirking their duties."

Sitting with proper posture was difficult as the weight of all he must give to the title and estate rested heavily upon his shoulders. He fought the desire to slump in his chair. He resisted the urge to argue with his mother. He'd known marriage was part of his role and he'd accepted it long before that moment. What he hadn't expected was arriving at this point in life without the proper plan to woo the woman he wanted to marry. He'd thought it would be easier than constant bickering and slinging insults like snowballs.

"Poor Miss Atkinson and all the other women who have set their caps on you. The disappointment will be jarring." Oliver's voice echoed through the emptiness in Baxter's head. "Will you marry before Phineas and Cornelius leave?"

Baxter looked to the end of the table where Cornelius sat. "You are leaving? When?"

Cornelius slowly turned his head his mouth agape in disbelief toward their youngest brother. Growling at the brother who had turned twenty only three months previously, the military Captain shined through Cornelius's glare. "It was not to be announced in this way."

"Sorry, but I thought Baxter needed saving." Oliver's impertinent toothy grin set everyone except Cornelius to laughter.

"At my expense?"

Baxter was thankful for the lighthearted conversation that followed Oliver's announcement, but a turmoil of emotions battled within his stomach. He knew there was no way of preventing Cornelius from leaving with the military. So, he wouldn't expend energy upon the topic. Instead, he fought the urge to cast up his accounts as he realized everyone in the family now knew Gigi expected him to make a match. He only hoped they weren't aware that Gigi's choice sat next to him at the supper table.

When they entered the drawing room for after supper conversation, Baxter sat on the sofa near Miss Kensington. He leaned toward her; his curiosity piqued and his courage up. With a glass of port to settle his nerves, he was finally willing to make a fool of himself in front of his brothers to win Miss Kensington's heart and honor Gigi's request. "Miss Kensington, I truly enjoyed the song you performed last evening. Did your mother teach you to sing? Or were you trained by a governess?"

"You are too kind, my lord." He noticed her blush and waited for her to answer his question. "My mother was a terrible singer. She refused to perform even in the walls of our home. I had a vocal instructor for many years."

"You must sing for us again."

Miss Kensington smiled and blushed. "I would love to do so. Do you sing?"

Baxter nodded. "I do, but I have not performed for many years."

"Why ever not?"

"Oliver is very talented with musical instruments. We are generally content to allow him the recognition in public. Cornelius provides us with his vocals when in private. No one in the neighborhood knows of his talent."

"Do any of your other brothers sing? I noticed none of them performed during the musical."

"We were all trained on the same instruments as Oliver, and our talents on each vary. We also have varying vocal talents. If it would please you, I will convince Cornelius to sing for us."

"Please do." Her eyes went wide with excitement, and Baxter found himself wishing she would touch his arm with her delicate fingers as the women vying for his attention always seemed to do.

"Cornelius, I was speaking with Miss Kensington, and she told me she has yet to hear you sing. I thought it would be a perfect ending to the night to have you perform."

He knew Cornelius was not shy and he would gladly entertain them for the evening. Baxter watched Miss Kensington's face as Cornelius stood at attention, ready to sing. As Cornelius opened his mouth and let out the first chord, Miss Kensington's eyes went wide. She was genuinely shocked.

"How?" She was speechless, utterly incapable of forming the question he knew must be aching to burst from her mouth.

"I have absolutely no explanation for his talent. He came home from his tour to the continent with the ability to yodel and we have been entertained ever since."

As Cornelius finished singing, Baxter clapped along with everyone else. He hoped to continue his conversation with Miss Kensington, but much to his dismay, Mr. Hayes arrived for an evening visit. He wasn't about to make a fool out of himself in front of a neighbor, and so Baxter moved to his normal chair across the room.

Much to his surprise, Baxter noticed Miss Kensington seemed indifferent to Hayes, and it gave him a boost of confidence to see her eyes darting toward him throughout the night. It was even more surprising to see they were soft and quite possibly showing her bewilderment and disappointment over his change in behavior. He'd thrown her off balance, and he decided this first real attempt at courting Miss Kensington had worked.

Chapter Nineteen

The ruins stood in the distance beckoning her to walk toward them, but she knew Lord Grafton wouldn't welcome the impertinence of finding her own way to the edifice, and so she stayed in the warmth of Primrose Hall. Remembering his invitation to borrow books from the library, Briar walked through the quiet home slowly, thinking about what she would like to read.

In truth, she wanted to know about the history of the ruins. She wanted a written history instead of the lore passed down through the Fernley family. It was possible there was an embellishment or lost information on the fire, and the truth could be hidden within the shelves of the library, waiting for her to find it.

Determined to discover facts, Briar entered the library. Each shelf posed a possible resting place for the journals. Dilapidated leather-bound books with delicate bindings were mixed amongst shiny and newer looking models adorning each shelf, waiting for the casual passerby to pick one up and flip through its pages. It would take months to search through each shelf, so she decided to start with the books nearest to the door.

The natural morning light flowed through the window, allowing her to see without a candle. Every wall in the library was covered from floor to ceiling with books of varying thickness and size. Briar ran a finger along each spine as she read the titles. She wanted journals, personal histories, family histories, or a history on Yorkshire.

Much like the current Lord Grafton, the books were in perfect order. The first section contained books on mathematics alphabetized by author and then title. As she neared a cluster of brown leather chairs, she noticed the topic of books focused on estate management, animal husbandry, and crop rotations. It wasn't surprising to see these were near the chairs. She wondered if Lord Grafton had the room rearranged each time he studied a certain topic; it would make sense to move the chairs for a more pointed study of the subject. But, as these books would not help in her search, Briar moved past them.

The next section held every book she could ever imagine had been written on theology. Running her fingers along the spines, Briar noticed a gap, and she wondered if Gilbert spent much time in the library or if there was someone else at Primrose Hall who enjoyed studying topics on religion. She could look in the ledger near the door, but her curiosity was more focused on finding the journals than concern over who was studying religion.

Checking each shelf, Briar crouched low to make certain everything in the section was focused on the same topic, when her eyes caught on a row of large books. Each book was wrapped in paper to preserve the ancient material. There were no visible markings on the paper to tell her the topics, so Briar lifted the first one out. Carefully unwrapping the paper, Briar opened the first book to discover it was a family record with each member listed by order of birth. On the first page, the initial people listed held the Fernley name but not a title. Ronald Fernley and his wife Clara Adams with their eleven children were the first records given. Most of the children died soon after their births. Only two lived to adulthood and had spouses with children.

This was a start to the information she wanted. Making herself comfortable on the floor, Briar used her legs to prop the book up as she searched each page until she found the title and name of the first earl. His Christian name had been Paul Octavius Fernley. His wife and each of the children were listed by birth order. Again, she noticed there were several births with death dates soon after, especially the last child. The child whose death coincided with the death date of Julia, the first Countess of Grafton was simply called *Girl*.

This small piece of information led her to believe the story passed down through generations of Fernley's might have been accurate. Briar followed the history of the title, looking to each earl and his position within the family. As she looked upon the entry for the fifth earl, she noticed there were more than seven sons listed under Bradford Fernley and Georgiana Langford. They'd also had three daughters. Briar slowly read each name with reverence. Anna, Marianne, and Esther, the first two having died soon after birth. The memory of Lord Grafton's laughter when he'd spoken of Esther entered her mind as she noticed the date of birth for Esther was connected to the current Lord Grafton. The death date next to Esther would have made her seven years of age.

Briar didn't realize her hand was covering her mouth until the light from the window darkened and she looked up to see Lord Grafton and Gigi standing above her. Startled by their sudden appearance, Briar dropped the book, let out an embarrassing shriek, and then scrambled to her feet.

"Lord Grafton, Gigi, I did not hear you enter." Briar looked to the ground to see the book was laying haphazardly on the carpet.

Gigi gave her a warm smile, which helped ease the tension of being caught snooping. Although she'd been given permission to look at the books, she was certain the information she'd discovered was far too personal for what Lord Grafton had approved. He'd most likely thought she would find a book of poetry or fiction.

141

Gigi reached forward and took her hand. "We worried when you did not arrive for the morning meal. Have you been in here long?"

Shivering, Briar hadn't realized she was cold until Gigi's warm wrinkled hands covered hers. "I woke early, and since Lord Grafton gave me permission to borrow books, I came down to find—"

"Our family history?" Lord Grafton cut her off, finishing her statement with what sounded to be an accusation.

Briar gave him a disapproving glare. "I wanted to find more information on the fire that destroyed the original house. I admit, I am a bit obsessed with the ruins and the history surrounding them."

"It is an interesting part of our past, but I do not think your curiosity will be satisfied with these books." Gigi stepped over the book Briar had dropped and led her to a section of the library closer to the fireplace and another set of leather chairs. "The information we have on the fire can be found in a book on the history of Yorkshire and another one focused on the surrounding areas of Whitby. But, if you are looking for a more personal history, such as a journal, those books are over here." Gigi again pulled Briar to another section of the library, and she pointed to the journal that would give most of the information.

Lord Grafton cleared his throat, pulling her attention away from the shelves of history books and journals. She noticed he was carefully rewrapping the genealogical record to preserve the leather using the same paper she'd removed when she read it. "The personal journals of our family are not available for visitors to search through."

Fully rebuked by his statement, Briar felt the familiarity of heat rising in her neck up to her cheeks. As a visitor, she had overstepped, and it was unacceptable. She owed her hosts an apology. "I understand." She looked to the ground unable to meet his gaze. "I did not mean to pry into your personal business."

Gigi seemed to be less shocked and more accommodating than her son. "You may ask anything you would like about our family. We have nothing to hide, and I will gladly share our history with you."

"Thank you." She knew Gigi considered her to be part of the family, even if she wasn't related by blood. Briar allowed Gigi to lead her out of the library to the breakfast room where she quietly broke her fast. There were so many unasked questions about the Fernley family floating through her mind. After what she'd seen in that book, most of them surrounded the three daughters Gigi had lost, especially Lord Grafton's twin sister.

It was interesting to Briar to see the difference between her and Gigi's reactions to losing a loved one. Perhaps length of time, after a loss, would help bring more clarity to the pit of confusion she now felt, but it was difficult to understand how Gigi could accept Briar as a surrogate daughter after losing three of her own.

She knew Gigi wanted to be a mother figure in her life, and she was attempting to allow the woman the liberty of fulfilling that role, but there were moments of doubt in her heart, and emotionally, she still resisted the warmth of a motherly embrace. At that moment, she couldn't imagine ever allowing someone to take the place of mother or father, and the stark realization of never again seeing her mother and father left her lost.

UNSETTLED BY THE EMOTIONS WELLING UP INSIDE, BRIAR didn't follow Gigi into the morning room to visit with neighbors. Knowing Mr. Hayes would be there, she couldn't take herself into the room to sit and listen as he spoke about the same topics over and over. She wanted to be alone so she could miss her parents without having to explain her feelings, and so she climbed the stairs and walked back to the portrait gallery.

Portraits of people no longer living covered the walls, and it seemed the appropriate place to think about her parents. When leaving her home in Boston, Briar had wanted to take every part of her life with her, but she'd been unable to do so. Their portraits had been packed and stored. She did have a small likeness of her parents that she was able to carry with her as they were miniature paintings, but they were nothing like having her mother and father available for conversation.

When Lord Grafton had shown her the portrait gallery, she hadn't noticed much of anything outside of the people he'd pointed to and the first earl. This time, as she entered the hall, she walked directly to the portraits of those yet living. Somehow, she knew there would be a portrait of Lady Esther.

The portraits hadn't been updated for many years, but she could tell who each of the Fernley boys were because they hadn't changed much as they'd aged. The portrait of Lord Grafton was newer, likely commissioned since he'd taken on the role of earl. She wondered whose portrait would hang next to the current Lord Grafton once he finally took a wife.

The conversation of the previous night played through her mind as she remembered his concentrated glare toward Gigi. It was obvious he hadn't wanted anyone to know she'd discussed a marriage arrangement with him.

Briar initially recoiled at the idea of Lord Grafton marrying anyone. It wasn't that she didn't think him worthy of a marriage, it was more a sense of loss on her part. She was attracted to her protector, far more than she wanted to admit, but she didn't love him. Although, he'd told her love was not necessary for marriage.

She was certain if he announced a marriage any time soon, it would be out of a sense of duty. He would honor Gigi's choice for a daughter even if he wasn't in love with the lady. Her heart ached for all Lord Grafton would miss emotionally. Although she'd never been in love, she had read about the euphoria of a pounding heart and the pleasure of a kiss. The safety of being with someone who cared about the other's well-being invoked desire within her heart. She was certain an arranged marriage couldn't lend such emotions.

Shaking away the sorrow for Lord Grafton's future marriage, Briar looked to the current portrait next to Lord Grafton to see a little girl who would forever be young in the eyes of those who knew her. She couldn't have been more than five years of age when the painting had been completed. Guilt spread through her chest as she realized she had taken the place of Gigi's daughter. It didn't seem right.

"I thought I would find you here." For the second time that morning, Briar let out a shriek after being startled. She turned to see Lord Grafton's eyes narrowed in suspicion. "Is this what you found so shocking in our family pedigree?"

"I thought it surprising no one has ever mentioned you are a twin. Not even you told me as much when you mentioned stealing sugar plums with Esther."

Lord Grafton's eyes raised up to his sister's portrait, and she was surprised to see a pleasant smile had returned to his face. He wasn't stuck in a pained half attempt at pleasure like when she annoyed him. The memory of his sister seemed to bring peace. "We do not speak about Esther often, but when we do, the memories are ones of joy."

"She was very young when she passed away. Was it sudden?"

"May I ask you a question, Miss Kensington?"

She'd invaded his privacy over the past few hours; there was no reason for her to deny him. "If you must."

"When people ask you about your parents' death, do you enjoy sharing the details?"

This caught her off guard, and her emotions welled up inside. She didn't want to argue with Lord Grafton, and so she allowed the tears to trickle down her cheeks. She didn't answer him but accepted the handkerchief he offered.

"I find Americans are overly curious when it is inappropriate. No one in all of England would have asked such a question, out of respect for my family, but you did. It is all very interesting to you, and you show little to no regard for our feelings." Lord Grafton continued speaking. "My sister had an infection of the lungs. It was a long and painful death. It is not something we speak about."

Ignoring his slight on her nationality, Briar decided it would be best to offer her apologies. "I should not have asked."

"No, you shouldn't have." Lord Grafton turned from the portrait to look at her, Briar was thankful he didn't look angry. "But I find curiosity is in your nature, and you are not to be persuaded once you have made up your mind. So, tell me, what did you discover in your research this morning that has you so unraveled?"

He'd answered her questions, so it was only right to confide in him. "When Gigi asked me to refer to her with the name her children use, she made me feel like I was a daughter to her. Now I realize she had three daughters, and I was presumptuous in my thinking."

"I cannot understand why you think this way. Gigi has accepted you into our family, and I know she loves you as a daughter."

Briar shook her head in frustration. He was not understanding her concern. "It is wrong for her to replace her daughters with me. I do not understand how she can overcome the loss of a child and accept another."

Lord Grafton's eyes went wide with her confession, and she feared she'd said too much. "Miss Kensington, she is not replacing my sisters. Gigi's heart is a mother's heart. She has enough room for more people to love. Love for family does not work in the way you are describing. It is not possible to replace a person. We will never replace my sisters, and we will never replace my father, even if Gigi loses her mind and marries another man."

Briar didn't know why his statement hit her as funny, but she giggled through the tears and accidently snorted when she tried to stop. To her utter embarrassment, Lord Grafton's eyes lit up and he burst into laughter with her.

"Why are you laughing?" Briar asked, as she calmed herself.

"You snorted."

Playing coy, Briar gave him her most innocent pout. "I did not. You must have heard wrong."

"You did, and that is why your face is bright red."

Briar placed her hands over her cheeks to cover her blush. "If I admit to snorting, will you promise never to tell another soul?"

Lord Grafton stopped laughing and with sincerity, he placed his hand over his heart and bowed his head. "I promise as a gentleman to never divulge what I heard."

With the agreement in place, Briar took Lord Grafton's arm and allowed him to escort her out of the portrait gallery. The short discussion with him helped her understand a little more about loss and grief. One day, she might be able to fully accept Gigi as a surrogate mother without forgetting her mother and the life she'd lived.

Chapter Twenty

"Miss Kensington, will you join me for a ride?" Baxter hoped to take Briar away from Primrose Hall and allow her time to process the feelings unearthed during her morning in the library. He also wanted to share part of himself with her so she could come to know the side of him that was passionate, caring, and relaxed.

Her face lit up with excitement, and he knew he'd made the right decision. He'd never been the one to bring such a beautiful smile to her face, and it felt like a triumph to see it now. "Will you take me to the ruins?"

He couldn't deny her request, and he had to admit the thought of sharing the ruins with her after such an amenable morning felt right. "Yes. You will want to dress warmly."

Baxter walked her to the bottom of the stairs and arranged to meet her on the hour. He ordered the sleigh and then entered the morning room to greet their guests. Although he wouldn't stay for a long visit, it was appropriate to thank the neighbors for visiting. He was surprised to find Mr. Hayes amongst his brothers, and he wondered if Miss Kensington was aware of the man's presence in their home. He worried she would cancel their carriage ride upon finding Hayes was there for a visit.

"Baxter, I thought you were occupied with the estate this morning." Gigi pointed to a chair across the room, but he waved the gesture off.

"I will not be here long. I thought we had actual guests." Mr. Hayes was always at Primrose Hall, and although Baxter hadn't meant it to sound like a rebuke, it had come out that way.

Mr. Hayes laughed, obviously not understanding Baxter's meaning. "Grafton, your sense of humor astounds me. Whenever I expect you to be in a serious mood, you make comments intended to bring out my blush."

"There is no need to resort to such awkwardness." Baxter was thankful Ames entered the room and offered him his gloves and hat.

"Miss Kensington is ready, my lord."

"Miss Kensington is in the hall?" Hayes asked. He stood and made a show of peering out of the door. "I thought she was indisposed today."

Baxter nodded to Ames, letting him know he appreciated the information. Looking back to Mr. Hayes, Baxter had a pleasantly wicked smile upon his face as he informed the man of his plans. "Miss Kensington has agreed to accompany me on a ride."

"Oh?" Hayes's flustered movements left Baxter even more pleased with the situation. Hayes was good company most of the time, but he was not a good match for Briar.

Baxter fully intended to help Briar see himself as a suitor instead of Hayes. The thought left Baxter a little off balance, but he recovered as Miss Kensington entered the room. "You said to meet on the hour, did you not?"

"Yes, I am sorry for my delay." Baxter held his hat in one hand as Ames helped him with his coat.

"Miss Kensington, if you wanted to take the air, I would have accompanied you." Hayes stepped forward offering his arm. "It is not necessary to bother Grafton. He has much on his mind with the estate and his duties as magistrate. Why, only yesterday I heard young Timothy Donner and Miss Mary James were seen sneaking off into the woods for a private tête-à-tête. Their parents will not be happy with the progression of their friendship after the scandal of that letter."

Baxter put his hand up to stop Hayes from continuing his speech. "There is no need to worry about my duties, and a magistrate need not interfere with young love. I decided to take the air, and I asked Miss Kensington to accompany me. It is a purely selfish outing on my part as I did not want to ride on my own."

Hayes obviously didn't think the conversation was over. As Baxter offered his arm to Miss Kensington, Hayes's apprehension increased. He rushed forward to block their exit from the room. "Miss Kensington, it is a cold day out. Would you not prefer staying by the fire? I read a new book on the history of the colonies last night, and I thought you would be interested in discussing the Articles of Confederation."

Miss Kensington looked to Baxter, and he feared she would back out of the ride. Mr. Hayes was a determined suitor, and he had paid attention to Miss Kensington when Baxter had not. He suddenly feared he'd misread the connection they'd shared while in the portrait gallery. He worried she didn't want to discover if there could be a friendship and possible courtship between them. When she spoke, his heart fell, and then he experienced an overwhelming sense of relief. "Thank you, Mr. Hayes, I would be delighted to hear what you have to say at another time. I agreed to take the air with Lord Grafton today, and I am invested in this trip."

He repeated the word, *invested*, in his mind as he walked her out to the sleigh. He was elated to know she would like to spend time with him. He made certain everything was proper. A trusted maid sat next to the driver while he and Miss Kensington nervously occupied the bench next to each other with blankets and a hot brick to prevent the cold from seeping through their outerwear.

He could pretend his leg bounced due to the cold, but it was a nervous habit. "The snow is still quite deep up by the ruins. I hope you will not be disappointed if we cannot get in."

Miss Kensington bit her bottom lip and tilted her head to look at him with pleading eyes. He waited for her to speak, his heart pounding loudly in his ears. "I am daring enough to walk through snow, my lord. Please do not think I will be happy sitting in the safety of the sleigh when I will be so close to the magnificent edifice adorning the landscape from my window. If you did not want me to become obsessed with the place, you should have assigned me to rooms on the opposite side of the hallway."

Baxter knew if she had said such an impertinent comment weeks before, he would have held it against her, but he now found it endearing. "You would trample through the snow to satisfy your curiosity?"

"Yes. And I dare you to try and stop me."

Baxter held up his hands in surrender. "I dare not, Miss Kensington. That gleam of adventure in your eyes makes me believe you will achieve your goal of visiting the inside of the ruins before spring, if not today."

"Is it lovely inside?"

Baxter considered her question. He'd seen the ruins so many times, and yet he was constantly amazed at the beauty within. "Yes, right now it is covered in snow, but in the spring, there will be a bed of wildflowers in every color."

"Will you allow me to go there in the spring?"

Baxter turned to Miss Kensington. He hoped he would be the one escorting her to the ruins each time she went. "If you would like me to take you there, I would be honored."

Miss Kensington looked into his eyes, and she smiled. "I think I would like that."

Baxter's mouth fell open in absolute shock. The simpleness of her statement left him reason to hope there could be a future for them. There was no angst or hatred within her eyes. Nothing vexing upon her tongue. They were sitting in the warmth of a sleigh sliding along the frozen earth to share an amiable afternoon together.

"Lord Grafton, why do you go out to the ruins so often?"

"When I am sitting atop the walls, I can hear the echo of life around me. The snapping of a twig as a rabbit runs past or the chirping of birds. The wind carries the joyous cries of children from the village as they laugh and play in the fields. I can enjoy the elegance of the ocean in the distance as the sun reflects off the surface. It is a place where everything seems perfect, and I can take in the beauty surrounding me."

"Is it a religious experience for you?"

Baxter considered her question, and then agreed. He was sharing far more than he'd expected with Miss Kensington, and he wondered how she had drawn the information out of him. "I believe so. I feel peaceful when I am there, much more than I do while sitting in the pew at church on Sunday."

"I will not tell Gil you prefer the outdoors to the church." Miss Kensington smiled conspiratorially at him, causing Baxter to laugh.

"Where do you go for peace?" He wanted to turn the conversation away from himself and find out more about the woman sitting next to him.

"I have not discovered any place since I arrived in England. But when I was at home in Boston, I would sit on the veranda with a cup of tea and watch the sunset."

"Do you miss Boston?"

Briar eyes glazed with nostalgia as she spoke. "Very much. I miss my home and my parents. I miss the companionship of comfortable friendships made over my lifetime. I miss everything I once had, and I fear I will never find it again."

"You miss belonging somewhere?"

"Yes."

Her words left him regretful for everything he'd ever said about her being an American. When he hadn't known her, she'd represented a people he despised for their lack of loyalty to the crown. He'd assumed all Americans were ungrateful for the land they'd been given by the king. Prisoners who weren't welcome in England and Scotland had been shipped to the Americas, and therefore many of the people who roamed free upon that land were descendants of thieves and murderers. But this beautiful woman sitting next to him wasn't as uncultured as he'd originally convinced himself. She was kind and caring and full of pain.

Baxter allowed her to speak of her friends whom she missed, as he helped her down from the sleigh and they trudged through the snow up to the ruins. He listened, and a part of him wished he could meet her friends. When they approached the arch that had once held two large double doors, Baxter stood back and allowed Miss Kensington to enter on her own. She'd longed for this moment, and he wanted to give her a chance to see it without him blocking her view.

Walking behind her, he smiled as she removed her gloves one finger at a time to touch the broken stones and crumbling bricks. She visibly shivered as wind howled through the corridor where they stood, but she didn't seem to mind the weather. There wasn't any snow in the tunnel that had once been a hallway; instead it was filled with decaying ancient cobblestones and mud. She stopped before walking out of the tunnel, and her ungloved hand went over her mouth. Miss Kensington took a moment to look around before turning back to him. "You didn't tell me it was magnificent. You only said beautiful."

Baxter chuckled. "I did not realize there was a difference. Please forgive my oversight."

"This is magical." Although she was looking upon a haphazardly crumbling stone edifice, Miss Kensington's eyes were wide with the innocence of a debutante seeing a decorated ballroom for the first time. "I have never seen anything so wonderful."

To his surprise, Miss Kensington walked into a fresh pile of snow that had been untouched until she'd disturbed the flakes. She lay on her back and moved her arms up and down to make a snow angel.

When she was finished, Baxter helped her stand and assisted her with brushing the snow off her pelisse and bonnet. "Is it what you expected?"

"Much more, my lord."

He assisted Miss Kensington up the ancient crumbling steps to the top of the tower and stood next to her as she silently took in the land that he'd always considered his. It was his estate, and he was master of all of it, but sharing it with Miss Kensington was like giving her a piece of himself. Although he would never tell her as much, he knew as she reveled in the beauty of his land that he had to win her heart.

They stayed at the ruins until they were shivering, and then they slowly made their way back to the sleigh. He was content and happy to sit in silence as they traveled back to Primrose Hall. The brick was still warm enough to give off heat, but Miss Kensington shivered as she sat next to him. He wanted to put his arm around her and pull her into his side to share the little bit of warmth in his body, but he stopped himself from doing so. It would be inappropriate. Thinking over the last few hours, Baxter realized this was the longest time they'd spent together without an argument. Inwardly he was cheering as he counted this as a successful attempt at courtship.

BAXTER HUMMED AS HE WALKED THROUGH THE VILLAGE on his way to the official office for his position as magistrate. He'd spent little time there since his last judgement on Daniel Vanstone, and he needed to make certain everything was in order. Tipping his hat toward the local baker, Baxter called out a friendly greeting and continued toward his destination.

His morning trip to the ruins had left him hopeful for a future with Miss Kensington. Of course, it would take time, but with her grandfather on the continent, they had months to discover if they would make a good match.

"Lord Grafton, may I have a moment of your time?" Hayes stepped into Baxter's path, blocking Baxter from his destination.

Nodding his agreement, Baxter pushed forward. He wanted to finish his business in town and arrive home in time to escort Miss Kensington into supper. The memory of the warmth of her arm on his was enough to make him consider turning back and forgetting his duties as magistrate. "What is on your mind, Hayes?"

"I would like to know what your intentions are toward Miss Kensington."

Baxter was fully aware of Hayes's lack of manners, so he wasn't at all surprised by the question, but he was irritated. "I thought I was her protector, not you."

"You bring up a valid point, Grafton. As her protector, it is inappropriate for you to put her into the position of accepting your courtship. She will feel obligated, as she is under your care. You cannot rightly offer her a courtship until Mr. Kensington is back in Yorkshire and she is removed from Primrose Hall."

Baxter was fully aware of his duty and the impropriety of forcing a relationship on a woman under his care. He was not a cad, and he would be certain of Miss Kensington's feelings before offering marriage. "I will consider all you have said. Thank you for stopping by."

Nothing Hayes said would deter Baxter from courting Miss Kensington. Everything would have to be done with propriety, but he would not allow a presumptuous man in pink trousers to dictate the rules of duty and honor to him.

Chapter Twenty-One

"Miss Kensington, will you take a turn about the room with me?" Mr. Hayes gave an exaggerated bow that left Briar unsettled. Mr. Hayes had joined them for supper, and he'd clung to her side at every possible moment. She'd been relieved for the short time the men had stayed behind for port. The few minutes alone with Gigi had been refreshing.

Briar looked around the room for a way to escape Mr. Hayes. He was acting strangely. Catching Gigi's eyes, Briar tried to convey the desire to get away from Mr. Hayes by outright mouthing the word, help.

She was thankful when Gigi didn't hesitate. She took Briar's hand and looked to Mr. Hayes. "Forgive an old woman, Mr. Hayes, but I did ask Briar to sit with me."

Hayes bounced on the front of his feet, his hands rigidly clutched behind his back. "Certainly, you can visit another time. You have tomorrow for womanly chatter."

"I am sorry, Mr. Hayes, but I must insist."

Briar tightened her hold on Gigi's hand as she held her breath and waited for Mr. Hayes to decide his course of action. As he moved toward Archie, Briar allowed herself to let out the breath she'd with-held and suppress the anxious feeling in the pit of her stomach. Looking to Gigi, she owed her an explanation. "I am sorry to put you in such an uncomfortable situation of telling a falsehood. Please forgive my assumption at stealing your time this evening."

Gigi smiled indulgently. "I do not mind. But I am curious as to why you chose to turn Hayes away. I thought you enjoyed his company."

Briar looked down at their clasped hands, gathering her thoughts so she could explain her reticence. "I think very highly of Mr. Hayes and his kindness toward me. He has been attentive over the past month, but I am confused. I do not think it is fair for me to encourage him at this time."

Gigi gingerly caressed Briar's hand. "Do you want to speak about it?"

"Not yet." Every part of her heart was aching to confide in some-one, but what could she say? She'd had a lovely time with Lord Grafton during their visit to the ruins. But was one lovely afternoon enough to turn another man away, especially a man who had taken great pains over the last month to show her special attention? It seemed cruel to even consider another man, and she inwardly berated herself for allowing Mr. Hayes the hope of more than friendship.

Briar allowed her eyes to sweep across the Grecian rug to where she knew Lord Grafton sat reading a book. It was his nightly routine. He always sat in the same chair, and she wished he would find his way over to sit next to her, as he had previously. She didn't allow her eyes to look beyond the tips of his boots as her heart fluttered in her chest, and she wondered if he was looking at her.

The kindnesses he'd shown her while at the ruins and in the carriage had to mean something, and she had entertained every possible argument for and against gaining his affections. In the end, she was left confused, especially because she knew he must marry the woman Gigi had requested.

Looking back at Gigi, she noticed the woman had silently watched each of Briar's movements, yet she kept a motherly expression of support upon her face. There weren't any assumptions, nor was there disappointment or shock. She simply looked like the trusting woman Briar had come to know and love. Briar dared not hope Gigi had asked Lord Grafton to marry her. It would be too wonderful and far too frightening.

"When you are ready, I am willing to listen."

It was nice to have someone she could rely upon as a confidante, and since Gigi wasn't trying to push her into speaking, Briar felt more of a kinship to the woman. She needed time to sort through her feelings for Lord Grafton. She'd spent so much time despising him, it was difficult to think of him as anything but odious. All she knew at that moment, was during the few times they'd been alone together, he'd been exactly what she'd expected from a gentleman, and she had completely misjudged the man.

Needing peace and quiet to sort through her conflicting emotions, Briar stood, and as usual every man in the room did the same. "If you will excuse me, I think I am ready to retire for the evening."

Mr. Hayes crossed the room, concern for her evident in his outstretched hands. "Are you unwell?" Turning to Lord Grafton, Hayes continued. "Grafton, send for a physician. Miss Kensington looks sickly."

Briar looked past Mr. Hayes and met Lord Grafton's gaze. As she did, she realized it had been a mistake. His distress was evident, and it sent a flutter of butterflies in her stomach. "I am perfectly well, my lord. There is no need for a physician." Turning back to Mr. Hayes, she took a step away from him. She didn't want him taking her hands or offering comfort when it wasn't wanted. "Mr. Hayes, I thank you for your concern, but it is not needed. I have simply outdone myself today and would like to rest."

"You would tell me if you were unwell?" Mr. Hayes asked. Briar felt a prickle of shame at his continued expressions of concern. Her reasons for leaving the room were to think about a different man and to find peace away from Hayes. "Do not hide an illness. If the outing with Lord Grafton has left you unwell, then I will never forgive the earl."

Briar wanted this overexaggerated interlude to end. Hayes was making her out to be a fragile female, and although she was female and did need assistance at times, this was not one of them. "Thank you, Mr. Hayes, but there is no need for concern. I simply want to retire early."

Mr. Hayes made one last request before she left, which sent her into a panic. "Miss Kensington, I would like to request a private audience with you on the morrow. I will be here for the morning visit."

Briar gave a clumsy curtsey and found her way out of the room and up to her bedchamber. She walked without thinking about the direction she was headed, ignoring her surroundings. He wanted a private audience, she knew exactly what the request meant, and she wasn't ready for any man to offer for her hand. She certainly wasn't ready for Mr. Hayes to do so. If she hadn't insisted on being well, she might feign an illness in the morning, but she knew delaying the moment with Mr. Hayes would not change his mind. She would have to meet with him, and she would have to decide upon her answer.

WHEN MR. HAYES ARRIVED FOR THE PRIVATE conversation, Briar hadn't any idea how to respond to the question she knew he was about to ask. He had good qualities. Many of his qualities were suitable for a happy marriage, but at that moment, she couldn't think of any of them. The only thought pressing upon her nerves was how to refuse a man so inwardly focused. It was likely he wouldn't even hear her if she tried to refuse him.

As she walked with Mr. Hayes, her stomach churned with the small portion of eggs she'd forced down. She regretted eating anything for the morning meal and was thankful she'd left the bread alone.

"Miss Kensington, I admit I hoped to have a particular conversation with you today." Mr. Hayes insisted on holding her arm in his, so she kept her eyes on the path ahead. She didn't respond, which allowed Mr. Hayes to continue speaking. "Over the past weeks, I feel we have formed a bond of friendship and a relationship of love."

Briar didn't agree. She was most certainly not in love with Mr. Hayes.

"I believe we can build a happy life together. Once your grandfather returns from France, I intend to ask for his permission to marry you."

"Mr. Hayes, that is very kind of you. But I need time to consider my feelings, and I would prefer you not speak to my grandfather until I have made a decision."

Mr. Hayes frowned. He stopped walking and moved away from her. "I was under the impression you enjoyed our time together. Have I been mistaken?"

"You are not mistaken." She had enjoyed a friendship with him, but there was much more to marriage than what she currently felt. "I have not taken time to examine my heart, and I must be true to myself if I am to accept an offer of marriage." She didn't understand why she'd been able to refuse Oliver so easily but had a difficult time saying the words to Mr. Hayes. In truth, she already knew she didn't want to marry him. Prolonging the conversation would only make matters worse.

"I see." Mr. Hayes turned back toward Primrose Hall. "Is Lord Grafton the reason you have refused my offer?"

Technically, Briar hadn't refused him. She had requested more time to consider her feelings. But she couldn't deny the growing admiration for Lord Grafton, no matter how confusing it was. "I cannot say."

Hayes turned away and looked off into the distance. "You are not the first woman to fall prey to his charming flirtations. His title is heavily sought after by the women in Yorkshire and London, but I fear only one woman will be successful with Lord Grafton, and she will be titled. Most likely the daughter of a duke or marquess."

Knowing his words were a result of her hesitation at accepting his offer of marriage, Briar chose not to take offense at his callous remark. "Mr. Hayes, I assure you I am not looking for a titled husband. I simply need time to consider my feelings. I beg of you to consider my position. I am new to this country, and I know very few people. I need time to sort through my feelings. My grandfather has yet to return from the continent, and I would prefer to wait for an offer of marriage until he is here to give his blessing."

"Is it my clothing you do not care for? Perhaps my inability to stop speaking? You would not be the first woman to turn me away for my imperfections." His voice shook with the pain of rejection.

Briar looked down at the muddy path and noticed the hem of her dress had skirted the ground, leaving it a mess. She wished they were speaking about the weather instead of the gut-wrenching conversation on marriage. "Mr. Hayes, I cannot deny that those are two of your attributes I have not reconciled, and they will weigh heavily within my decision."

"When can I expect your answer?"

"I am unsure." Was it appropriate to put a timeframe on making such a life-altering decision?

"I will escort you home."

She hadn't expected the abrupt end to their outing, but in her current state of confusion over her budding feelings for Lord Grafton and Mr. Hayes's offer of marriage, Briar decided it was best. When Mr. Hayes left her in the entryway, Briar chose to take a walk in the gardens to clear her mind and think about everything she knew of Mr. Hayes.

The earth around her was still covered in the purest white snow. There were no flowers to enjoy, but it was a peaceful place to walk, and since she was alone, she didn't need an escort. As always, her eyes focused on the ruins in the distance, and Briar's thoughts turned to the relationship between the first earl and countess. She wished Lord Grafton would relent and allow her to read the journals from that time so she could know what had happened.

Lord Grafton had occupied her mind, and each time she tried to focus on another topic, she always came back to him. She could despise him for not allowing her to read the journals, but a small part of her understood his reasoning. She wasn't a true part of the family, and so the personal histories were not any of her concern.

"Briar, take care!"

Briar turned as she heard the words, but instead of seeing which of the six Mr. Fernleys had called out to her, she found a ball of snow flying through the air right before it landed on her shoulder. Stunned for only a second, Briar moved to action. She hadn't played in the snow since she was a child, and although she had a lot to consider, she could delay for a moment of fun. She laughed and ran to the nearest edge of lawn to gather snow; whoever had thrown the pack of snow that was now on her pelisse would pay for it.

"Who threw that?" Briar called out.

Lord Grafton sheepishly stepped forward. "Miss Kensington, I do apologize for my poor aim. I intended to hit Phineas."

"Then I do believe this belongs to you." Briar threw her perfectly formed snowball at Lord Grafton and laughed with Phineas as it smashed against Lord Grafton's chest. Before he could respond, Briar ran through the snow as it crunched beneath her boots. A snowball flew by the side of her arm, catching her pelisse and leaving a smear as she stooped down to gather more.

She knew targeting Lord Grafton would be flirtatious, but in this wildly improper moment, Briar let go and allowed the child within to be reckless. She threw another snowball and missed Lord Grafton as he weaved around bushes and trees.

"Phineas, help me!" Briar screamed as Lord Grafton sent two consecutive snowballs toward her.

"Do not fear, Briar. I will defend your honor."

Forming a truce with Phineas was the perfect solution to her poor aim. She used him as a shield as Lord Grafton threw snow from behind a tree. Briar couldn't stop the girlish giggles from escaping until a snowball hit Phineas in the nose.

"I think I have been rendered unconscious." Phineas fell to the ground and lay on his back.

"Phineas, you fought hard. Do not give up now." Briar formed another snowball and threw it at Lord Grafton, giving Phineas time to sit up and retake his position as shield.

She threw another snowball, and then jumped out of the way as Lord Grafton returned with three consecutive snowballs. As Phineas sat up, each of the balls hit him, and he went back down. "I think I am now dead."

Unable to stop laughing, Briar took his arm and meant to drag his body to safety, but he was too heavy. In between giggles, she managed to leave Phineas with parting words. "I am sorry, you will have to wait out the fight here. Stay down."

As Phineas feigned death and fell back into the snow. Briar took refuge behind a tree. In an effort of stealth, Briar peeked out only once she had a new ball of snow to release. To her surprise, before she could release the first of her snowball reserves, Lord Grafton ran forward and picked her up off the ground and then they both tumbled into the snow.

Briar giggled with further delight. She hadn't expected Lord Grafton to let go of himself so completely. As she lay in the snow, attempting to catch her breath, she looked into Lord Grafton's eyes and saw desire. It was a ludicrous thought, but as she saw the depths of the blue ocean before her, she was certain he was as confused as she was about the emotions welling up between them. A light ringing sounded in her ears as the world around her stopped moving. His arms felt right, his face so near hers was perfect, and she didn't want the moment to end without him placing a kiss on her lips. As she thought about lifting her head in his direction, fear overcame her emotions and she wanted to get as far away from the man as possible. Unfortunately, her body wouldn't respond. She lay frozen on the earth in a state of confusion, knowing if she made any movement toward him, he would kiss her.

"Baxter, have you lost your mind? You cheated," Phineas called out, breaking through the silent moment.

Lord Grafton's arms released her. The warmth of his embrace and the magic and stillness of the moment were gone as her mind registered the cold snow-laden ground beneath her. Briar scrambled to sit and move away from the earl. It was inappropriate for them to be in such a compromising position. She turned away as heat rose in her neck and cheeks. Taking Lord Grafton's offered hand, Briar stood, curtsied, and left for her bedchamber but not before she mumbled a ridiculous apology for behaving inappropriately.

BRIAR'S HEART FLUTTERED, AND SHE COULDN'T STOP smiling. Lord Grafton had nearly kissed her. She hadn't realized she wanted him to kiss her until it had nearly happened. Now, it was all she could think about as Lady Grafton and her maid helped her out of the wet clothing and forced her into a hot bath and then bed.

"I will speak to my son about the impropriety of throwing snow at a lady." Gigi piled three heavy blankets on top of Briar while she bemoaned her son's lack of manners. "If you catch your death from his little game, I will never forgive Baxter."

"There is no need to worry, Gigi. I will be warm before the night is out, especially with all of these blankets."

Gigi gave her an indulgent smile then turned to the maid. "I want two heating pans brought in, tea, and more wood to build up the fire."

Briar wanted to spend the day speaking with Lord Grafton. She wanted to know everything about him, even the things he'd never told another living soul. She wanted to understand his heart. More importantly, his dreams and desires.

"You would think an earl would have more sense than to throw a woman into the snow. Trust me, Briar, my son will receive a tongue lashing for his behavior."

"Do not be so upset with him. I engaged in the activity, and it was enjoyable."

Gigi stopped fidgeting and sat on the edge of the bed. "You are not offended by his actions?"

"I thought the morning enjoyable. It allowed me to clear my mind and think of something other than my current worries."

"You have been overwhelmed of late. I can see it in your face. Is there anything I can do to help you?"

Briar knew Gigi's words came from a desire to help, and she wanted to speak about the offer from Mr. Hayes with her, but was it appropriate? If Gigi were her mother, she wouldn't hesitate to share her concerns. "It is the type of problem I would have gone to my mother over."

Gigi nodded. "I understand. There are times a young woman needs the help of those who can lovingly embrace them. If you are willing to confide in me, I would like to try."

"Mr. Hayes requested my hand in marriage today." She'd thought to say more, but the words wouldn't form. They were far too difficult to speak, and she wondered if that was indicative of how she truly felt toward the man.

"I have watched you with Mr. Hayes, and I am uncertain as to how you feel about him. Do you want to marry him?"

Briar sat up and shivered as the blankets fell from her shoulders. She quickly scooted back against the pillows and pulled her legs up to her chest while Gigi repositioned the covers. "I am very aware of how I do not feel. I am not in love with him. I cannot deny that he is a good man, despite his tendency to talk all the time and his horrid sense of fashion."

"It sounds as if you have already made your decision."

Briar shook her head. How could she admit her concerns without sounding callous? "I have come to the realization that he is the only man attempting to court me, and I cannot continue to rely upon Lord Grafton's charity while my grandfather is away. My grandfather wants me to marry so he won't have to be concerned over my welfare, and this is the only opportunity I have, and so I fear I must accept."

Sharing her concerns had allowed the heaviness of the decision to lift a little. But she hadn't any idea how to accept marriage to a man she didn't love. Perhaps over time, she would find a way to love Mr. Hayes, but it would take adjustments on her expectations for a relationship.

She wished Gigi wouldn't respond, as the door to Briar's bedchamber opened and a maid entered with the wood for the fire. Another brought in the heating pans. And then a third brought in tea. As the maids went about their work, Gigi offered her advice. "Do not accept Mr. Hayes out of fear for your situation at Primrose Hall. My son takes his duty seriously, and he will not leave you in the cold without a place to go. You are welcome to live here for the rest of your life, even if you are unmarried."

It was kind of her to say as much, but visitors were known for wearing out their welcome. Briar refused to be the person who stayed too long. Such people usually caused discord for the host and his family. "Even an uncultured American understands propriety when it comes to house visitors. When Lord Grafton marries, the new Lady Grafton will not want me here."

Gigi smiled and took Briar's chin in her hand. She held onto Briar's face until their eyes met. "Promise me you will not accept Mr. Hayes out of fear. If you do accept his offer, do so because you want to be his wife."

"I will take more time to think about it."

Briar was thankful for the heating pans and the added warmth of the fire. As she lay in bed sipping the hot tea and absorbing the warmth and comfort Gigi and the maids offered, Briar tried to imagine a future with Mr. Hayes. The images wouldn't form in her head, and when she thought of marriage, the man next to her wasn't dressed in outrageous pantaloons and foppishly tied cravats. Instead, he was rigid and stiff and sometimes covered in snow. But most importantly, he was standing in the ruins with her, and she knew it would never be Mr. Hayes.

Chapter Twenty-Two

Baxter stood by the window looking out over his land. He preferred to ignore his mother—she was far too perceptive —and he hadn't any answers, or at least any to satisfy her queries. The only thing he knew was his mind was focused on Briar Kensington, and he couldn't bring himself to think of anything or anyone else.

She hadn't left her chambers for supper the night before, which had left him uneasy and concerned over her health. Suddenly, his life no longer made sense. Nothing made sense unless she was nearby, but how did he express such emotions to his mother? He had difficulty formulating the thoughts, and speaking was far worse. Instead of actual words and sentences, he simply stood silent. In truth, the entire situation had him baffled.

And then there was the spectacle he'd made of himself when he'd purposefully thrown snow at her. He hadn't aimed for Phineas, that had been a lie. He only hoped his mother didn't know about the moment he'd tumbled into the snow and nearly kissed Miss Kensington.

"Have you nothing to say?"

He turned away from the snow-covered ground to sheepishly confess. "Mother, I know my behavior was improper—"

Gigi laughed. "Improper? Baxter, I have never seen you throw snow at a woman in all my life. Your father never behaved in such a manner, and until this moment, I could not imagine what had come over you."

"You are not angry?" He'd expected a lecture on propriety and honor. After all, he was Briar's legal protector until Mr. Kensington returned.

"I admit it is shocking to see you so taken by a woman you had decidedly hated, but you know I heartily approve of the match. I had hoped you would like her. I imagined you would take her as a wife on my request. But I never expected you would fall in love so quickly. Of course, I would prefer a courtship, but marriage by special license is acceptable. I implore you to seek Mr. Kensington's approval, which will give you time for banns to be read."

Baxter's voice took on a shrill tone as he repeated what he considered the most important part of his mother's lengthy statement. "Special license?"

"Yes. You cannot throw a woman into the snow in such a scandalous way and expect to go back to pretending nothing has occurred."

"I cannot marry Miss Kensington. She does not feel for me as I do for her. She has no training on how to run a British household. She has certainly never been taught the duties of a countess." Realizing he'd practically declared his feelings to his mother, Baxter turned back toward the window to hide his embarrassment.

Gigi stood and crossed the room and forced him to turn back to her. "You cannot hide your feelings from me. I am your mother."

"I will not force Miss Kensington into a match."

"I believe your behavior yesterday morning showed the opposite of your words. If anyone other than your brother and I had seen the way you held Briar in the snow, we would not be arguing over a special license or the banns. Gilbert would have performed the wedding ceremony before nightfall."

Baxter closed his eyes to calm his nerves. He cleared his throat and took a deep, calming breath before daring to open his eyes and meet his mother's narrowed gaze. "You saw everything?"

"Yes. I never thought it possible of my very proper son."

Realizing the compromising situation he'd put Miss Kensington in, he backtracked on his feelings. A man who was in love would never compromise the reputation of the woman holding his affections. "Miss Kensington would be better off without me. I am still new in my role as earl. She deserves better than I can give her."

"I see. Then you will grant Mr. Hayes your blessing on a match, when he finally gathers the courage to speak with you as her protector?"

Baxter squirmed under Gigi's narrowed gaze. His mother was far too perceptive. He didn't know when he'd lost his heart to Briar, but he obviously hadn't hidden his preference as well as he'd hoped. He couldn't continue the pretense. "What am I to do? Declare my love and pray she feels the same for me?"

"What harm would it do?"

Baxter pulled away from his mother. "I am her guardian. It would be inappropriate for me to declare my intentions without knowing her heart."

"I have always believed we British can take honor a bit far at times. We have old traditions that a small amount of common sense could correct."

"She knows nothing of running a house like Primrose Hall."

"Fortunately, I have the ability to pass my knowledge on to her. You need not concern yourself over her training as a countess."

Baxter let out a sigh of frustration. "If I do not submit to the expectations of my position, then I am nothing. My title would mean very little if after generations of earls guarding the reputation of our family, I turn my back on propriety and decide the trust of my position can be so easily forsaken for personal gain."

"Oh, hush! You are speaking rubbish." Gigi took hold of his chin and forced him to look at her. "Matters of the heart are more important than titles, estates, and Society. If your father were here, he'd give you the same speech. Do not let Briar marry Mr. Hayes without telling her how you feel. Give her the chance to decide if she loves you as well."

"You cannot expect me to be less than what I am. You may believe I am too formal with my manners and desire for honor, but it is the way you and father raised me. It is all I know, and it is what defines me."

"I suppose the only question you need to answer then is, how will you spend the rest of your life knowing the woman you love has married another?"

Baxter turned back to the window. He was thankful the sky was dreary and grey. It was a perfect expression of how he felt. The thought of Briar marrying Hayes left him melancholy and empty. He didn't answer his mother. Instead, he stayed firm in his convictions, and he would not yield. His honor wouldn't allow it.

BAXTER SAT IN HIS FAVORITE CHAIR BY THE WINDOW WITH a book hoping to avoid after supper conversation. His erstwhile conversation with Gigi lay heavily upon his mind, causing him distress. Could he be a cad and openly court Miss Kensington while she lived under his protection? Would anyone in Society even notice? They were in Yorkshire, not in London. Even as he entertained the idea of a courtship, he knew word would spread through every parlor and gentleman's hall. Briar would be scorned amongst the elite unless he could find a way around his duty.

He could transfer her protection to Archie or Gil. Both would be perfect solutions for solving his problem, but did they want the burden of such a duty? He could ask Mr. Kensington to return to Yorkshire, but he didn't know what the situation was with the late Mr. Kensington's dealings in France. Overall, Baxter felt helpless to obtain his desire for courtship.

Settling against the chair for the night, Baxter planned to silently brood while his brothers, Mr. Hayes, Gigi, and Briar merrily chatted. He kept his book in the perfect position for him to see Briar across the room while he pretended to be distracted with reading. At least he hoped he was fooling everyone because it wouldn't be appropriate for him to watch as Hayes wooed Briar.

"Miss Kensington," Hayes announced, jumping to his feet in a show of surprise. "Please tell me you are jesting."

"I assure you, Mr. Hayes, I am in earnest."

As Baxter watched Hayes make a spectacle of himself, he wished he could be rude to his neighbor and refuse him entry to Primrose Hall. If he didn't allow Mr. Hayes to visit, then Hayes and Briar wouldn't form an attachment and his hand wouldn't be forced to a hurried courtship and finding her a new protector. It was the perfect solution.

"Hayes, what are you going on about?" Archie asked.

"Miss Kensington has only now admitted she has never danced a waltz. This revelation is too much for my sensibilities." Mr. Hayes held a hand over his chest in mock horror. The ridiculous man bothered Baxter to no end. Baxter didn't understand the foppish mannerisms and extreme fashions of the day, and in his frustrations over Briar, he allowed his annoyance with Mr. Hayes to intensify.

"Mr. Hayes, it is not so shocking for a woman of my age to have little experience with the dance. I have not yet received an introduction to Society here in England, and my mother wanted me to wait until my twentieth year to attend functions in Boston. Unfortunately, my parents passed before my debut."

"I must teach you tonight." Hayes took hold of Briar's hand and pulled her to her feet. Baxter grumpily rolled his eyes and pressed further into his chair. He didn't care to watch Hayes and Briar dance. He'd seen the two of them together at every Societal function over the past month. "Oliver, can you pound out an appropriate tune?"

"Mr. Hayes, I do not think it appropriate for a quiet evening. I would prefer to pass the night in friendly conversation." Briar pulled her hand from Hayes and turned to retake her seat.

Hayes took hold of her arm and pulled Briar away from the sofa. "Miss Kensington, I must insist. You cannot enter Society without the basic knowledge of the waltz. What will you do when you find yourself at Almack's with permission to participate in the waltz if you do not know the steps?"

Briar again pulled away from him. "Mr. Hayes, please understand I have no intention of dancing this evening."

"Miss Kensington, I only wish to help you with a successful launch into Society. It is imperative you know how to waltz."

Fear crossed Briar's features as she again pulled away from Mr. Hayes. As her protector, Baxter had to put an end to the display between them. As the man who loved her, he was ready to take Hayes out to the barn and send him off with his horse. Clearing his throat, Baxter placed his book on the table beside his chair. "Hayes, Miss Kensington requested you leave her to a peaceful evening of conversation. There will not be a waltz at Primrose Hall this evening."

"I only wanted to teach her the finer points of the dance. Grafton, if you were to give your permission for me to teach Miss Kensington the steps, I would take her to the ballroom this instant. She will be ready for London by the end of this night."

Baxter turned to Briar. "Miss Kensington, would you like to learn how to waltz tonight?"

"No, my lord."

He didn't like that she still referred to him so formally, but he also didn't like that she hadn't given him permission to use her Christian name. It was one more reason to prove his convictions on honor to be correct. She wasn't comfortable around him. It didn't matter what his feelings were. If she didn't love him, then a declaration would mean absolutely nothing.

"Hayes, you will leave Miss Kensington alone until she asks for your assistance." Baxter waited for Hayes to release Briar's hand before going back to his book. Again, he didn't read anything but spent his evening focused on Briar while wishing he was the man who could bring a smile to her face and brighten her evening. Instead, his brothers and Mr. Hayes were the successful ones.

Chapter Twenty-Three

"Do you want a tray this morning?" Betty asked as she opened the drapes, allowing the morning sun to brighten the room.

Briar sat up with the warmth of the sun resting upon her face. "The sun is out?"

"Yes, miss."

"It seems like ages since the sun has been so bright." Boston had winter snowstorms and it often rained, but she still felt like the gloomy weather of England would take time to acclimate to. Rushing through her morning routine, Briar wanted to spend her entire day basking in the warmth, what little there would be, of the sun.

She skipped the morning meal, her excitement pulling her toward the door and out into the melting snow. She longed to spend the day walking along the mud-ridden paths while she considered her feelings for Mr. Hayes and his offer. She needed to make certain the answer she gave was what her heart could live with. Deciding she wouldn't go too far, Briar headed in a direction that would place the ruins in her view. She loved the picturesque scene it made to have them bathed in snow with the sun shining upon the walls. The sun was certain to rejuvenate her soul, and if it didn't, the excitement she felt at seeing the morning rays and the warmth upon her cheeks would leave her renewed.

Settling her mind upon the much-needed task of Mr. Hayes and his offer, Briar considered everything she knew about the man, and she was convinced he was far too attentive. He wanted her full attention so he could dazzle her with facts that meant absolutely nothing in the grand scheme of life. But she wondered if his incessant chatter would end once he was married. His wife would certainly not want to sit and listen to the endless streams of facts. If she were his wife, she would have to put an end to it. Perhaps if he had a journal to write all his findings in, he wouldn't need to carry on so.

At the last party they'd attended, she'd been hurt by his ability to forget she was near him. She'd tried to excuse herself so she could speak with Cornelius, but Mr. Hayes hadn't acknowledged her. Did he want a pretty wife to hang on his arm and build up his self-esteem without offering anything in return? He'd complimented her earlier in the evening, so he was capable of noticing others outside himself, but when he was busy with useless facts, he would forget about her.

She didn't like his need to overdress, and a wife would certainly be able to squelch such things about a man. She could discuss the situation with Mr. Hayes's valet and convince him to find less noticeable fabrics. If she could ignore his callous ability to forget she was around when he was excited about a topic, could she marry him and convince him to change? The plan seemed nearly perfect until she started wondering what attributes she had that Mr. Hayes would want to change. Surely her faults were not so egregious as his.

She thought over the reasons she'd decided the Fernley men were not suitable, and she knew within her soul she couldn't accept a marriage with Mr. Hayes. He was fine for an evening but soon wore upon her nerves. He was very pleasant to look at, if one could ignore the pink cravat and bright yellow pantaloons and orange waistcoat, and the long list of clothing that made the man a peacock could go on if she allowed it to.

As she walked along the mud-ridden path with melting snow dripping like rain from the trees, Briar entertained what her life would be like if she married Mr. Hayes. He did have good qualities, even amongst the negative. He was kind, flamboyant, and ridiculous, to say the least. It pained her to realize she somehow always had to throw a disparaging thought into the mix. She could see a future filled with parties. There would never be a dull moment because he would convince her to dance with him each night at their home. With everything she'd compiled in her mind, she knew a life with Mr. Hayes was not suitable for her temperament. She needed quiet moments of reflection, and Mr. Hayes would never allow her to find solace in the silence.

She found Mr. Hayes to be a contradiction. His clothing and behavior suggested he was ready for a party, but the facts he shared were dry and leaned toward boring. She wondered which side was the true Mr. Hayes, and with her decision made, she wondered how she would refuse his offer without injuring the man. She wanted a friendship with him, not a marriage.

As she'd made her final decision, her foot sank into the mud. The sucking noise as she yanked her booted foot out reminded her of the morning she'd first met Lord Grafton. She could now laugh at the horrified expressions upon his face as he'd taken in her ruined clothing when she'd fallen in the mud. Looking down at her hemline now, she realized the state of her dress was much the same as it had been when she'd run into the formidable earl. Her clothing was ruined, and yet, she was delighted.

Noticing a puddle ahead, Briar ran forward and jumped directly in the middle, forcing the water to splash, further destroying her dress, but she found a sense of peace in something so trivial.

The sun shining down on her face lent warmth and kept her moving forward. As Briar rounded the bend that would lead into town, she recognized Lord Grafton standing at a grave in the church-yard. Walking toward his position, Briar considered the man who was assigned as her protector. He'd saved her from an impromptu waltz the previous night. He'd nearly kissed her during their snowball fight. She blushed with the memory of his deep blue eyes as they'd rested on her lips. There was no doubt in her mind he'd wanted to kiss her as much as she had ached for it to happen.

She wondered, if they had met under different circumstances, and if he didn't dislike Americans so much, if they could have been friends from the start. When he'd helped with the charity baskets and had taken her to the ruins, she'd realized there was more to admire about the man than his handsome looks. His generosity in accepting responsibility for her care and never complaining about it, even when she'd made a complete nuisance of herself by arguing, spoke volumes.

Lord Grafton was well spoken and genuine. His commitment to his duty had once set her into a tirade of complaints, but she had softened toward that attribute, and she now admired the strength of character it took to remain steadfast when others around him mocked or refused to see the importance of his commitment.

She wanted a man who had the strength of character to keep promises without question. She'd never realized how important duty was until she'd met Lord Grafton. When she was near him, he made her want to scream and smile all at once. She realized she didn't despise him.

As she thought more about Lord Grafton, she knew within her soul as she stood at the kissing gate that he was the man she wanted to marry. She'd never made a list of qualities, not like her friends in Boston had done. She'd always imagined that when she found the right man, she would know him. And she'd been right. He stood a short walk away, and her heart ached with regret over what could have been. The desire to be near him took her through the gate and along the path to the grave marker where Lord Grafton stood. She wanted to apologize for all the vexing comments of the past months.

She wanted to tell him he was the man she'd been searching for, even if it wasn't the appropriate way of declaring one's intentions. She wanted him to know she held him in the highest esteem and then pray he would one day care for her as she did him.

"Lord Grafton, I hope I am not disturbing you." Now she was standing next to him, she faltered on what to say. She tried to push the inclination to blush back, but from the smile on his face, she knew it hadn't worked. This was the first time they'd been alone since they'd almost kissed, and she wondered if he felt as shy as she did over the situation. Now that she knew he was the man she would compare all other suitors to, Briar had a rush of emotions welling up inside. She wanted to shout her feelings from the top of the ruins but would need a horse to get there.

"Not in the least." Lord Grafton said as he stood to his full height. Briar looked at the headstone he'd knelt before. She needed to push aside her feelings and speak, otherwise he'd wonder if she'd lost her mind.

"Is this your father's resting place?" She ignored the snow on his knees and the wet material of his trousers. She'd never seen his clothing in any other state than pristine.

"Yes."

His one-word answer left her searching for something more to say. She understood loss. Having lost both her parents at the same time, she often found an inability to express how she'd been affected by their absence. She didn't want to ask the wrong question and start an argument about how she was inappropriately prying into his life. Briar decided it was best to speak from her heart. "I wish I had the ability to visit my parents' resting place."

When he didn't immediately answer, Briar worried she'd said the wrong thing. But she was thankful when after he took a moment to think, he spoke, and his voice was even toned. "I never considered how leaving your home included your parents' graves. It must be difficult."

The emotion in his statement reinforced her newfound admiration for the man. She'd never noticed his intense ability to care for others. "I try not to think about it. If I do, the sadness will consume me." Briar shielded her eyes against the sun as she looked at him. "Do you come here often?"

Lord Grafton nodded and stepped in the perfect position to provide shade. "There are moments I feel an overwhelming urge to speak with my father."

"Do you come here when you are confused?"

"Yes, but I never receive answers. He is as silent as the grave." Lord Grafton's lips twitched as he tried to hold back a smile.

Briar appreciated this side of Lord Grafton. The worry she'd carried with her into the cemetery was gone as he let a smile break through. "Sometimes, when I feel very lonely, I find the likeness I have of my parents, and I think about what they would say to me."

"What do you imagine they would say about your move to Yorkshire?"

"Father always wanted to bring mother and me to visit Grandfather. He was my grandfather's natural heir, and my parents often spoke about the necessity of living their later years in England. But they never imagined the scenario where I would be here alone."

"Now you are here, what do you think about your new home?"

Briar worried her response would break the unspoken truce and cause a rift between them. She hadn't yet settled into an actual home. Her grandfather had left her in the care of Lord Grafton far too quickly. She truly didn't feel like Kensington Park was home, and Primrose Hall would never be a home to her.

"I have not yet come to love the land you cherish. It will take time for me to find comfort here."

"I am sorry to hear this. I have a feeling I am partially to blame for your discomfort."

Before this moment, she would have blamed Lord Grafton for all the reasons she disliked living in Yorkshire, but he wasn't the cause. It was her circumstances that had left her unsettled. If she'd moved to England with her parents, there wouldn't be an overwhelming sorrow within her soul. "It is not the place that causes my heart to ache. It is the people who should be here with me, and yet are not."

She'd missed Boston, but she now realized it was because Boston was the last place she'd been with her parents. She could fully convince her mind to believe that if she traveled back to her home, they would be in the parlor waiting for her. But when reality set in, she knew it wasn't possible.

"Do you think you will ever come to love Yorkshire?"

Briar looked down at the headstone of the previous Lord Grafton. She truly didn't know how to answer the question. But she knew the unrest would have to one day be resolved. "I do not know what my future will be, and therefore I cannot give an adequate answer." Moving away from him, she decided their conversation had come to an end. "If you will excuse me, I would like to continue my walk."

Lord Grafton looked down at her muddy shoes and the hem of her skirts. She nearly laughed at his disappointment. "Miss Kensington, I will instruct your maid to have hot water ready upon your return to Primrose Hall."

She curtsied and smiled at the ever-proper earl. "I promise not to tell anyone I am your houseguest, my lord. I would not want them to think you are hosting a heathen."

A genuine smile of pleasure made his austere features inviting. "It is too late. The entire neighborhood is aware of our connection. I do not believe we will escape the censure of Societal gossip at this point."

Briar laughed. "Then I will have to make a point of jumping in every puddle I see from this point on."

She didn't wait for him to respond. Instead, Briar turned and made her way back to the path that would lead her through town.

ALTHOUGH THE SUN WAS OUT, IT HADN'T YET MELTED THE ice on the bridge over the frozen river. Briar sat with her legs dangling over the edge, looking out at the winding river and the trees dripping with water as though they were crying. Were the trees mourning winter in preparation for spring?

The conversation with Lord Grafton lingered in her mind. It was a nice change to have conversations after which he didn't leave her wanting to pack her bags for Boston. Everything about his demeanor had changed since she'd first met him. They'd shared personal parts of themselves without accusing the other of some sort of treachery, and Briar found herself longing for more moments of comfortable conversations with him.

Closing her eyes, Briar allowed her imagination to take over. She pictured herself and Lord Grafton sitting on the sofa in the library, pouring over the history of his family. His features were soft and welcoming, and they were in love. Forcing her mind to stay on the same path, she imagined a baby with Lord Grafton's blue eyes and his strong jawline. Once she'd allowed herself to dream about the man, it was difficult to find reality. She wanted Lord Grafton to court her and offer marriage. But deep down she knew it wouldn't happen. His mother had asked him to marry a specific woman. And she knew his honor would require full acceptance of the match.

As the sun dipped behind the clouds, Briar reluctantly pulled herself up from the bridge and walked back to Primrose Hall. She hadn't eaten anything yet, and it would be nearly supper when she returned. The day had been pleasantly quiet and had given her time to ponder and imagine. As she neared Primrose Hall, Briar reminded herself that the hope built into the harmless musings of a marriage to Lord Grafton would never be real, and so she tucked them away and planned to never entertain them again.

Chapter Twenty-Four

Baxter couldn't stop thinking about Miss Kensington's reaction when he'd noticed her skirts were drenched in mud. She hadn't blushed like a proper English woman would have. Instead, she'd been fully aware of the state of her skirts and felt no shame in his notice. Surprisingly, he found it refreshing, and a part of him wished he'd offered to accompany her as she walked.

While looking over the estate finances, Baxter whistled a jaunty Irish folk song. For the first time since his father's death, he didn't despise this part of his life. He found joy in allocating funds to improve the estate.

He spent the afternoon alone in his study, energized by the beautiful day and his encounter with Miss Kensington. His hopes for friendship might be possible, and if so, then over time it could lead to love.

They had both suffered tragedy, and sharing parts of themselves had broken the tension between them. He never thought it possible to bond with someone over the loss of a parent, but the vulnerable way they'd spoken had left him hopeful, and for the first time since he'd watched his father's casket lower into the ground, he no longer felt drawn to the cemetery. He wanted to share his concerns with Miss Kensington, and he dared to hope at some point she would desire the same.

Excited to see Miss Kensington again, Baxter impatiently waited for the afternoon to melt away so he could spend his evening with his family and the woman who was occupying his every thought and filling his life with meaning.

AS EVERYONE SETTLED INTO THE PARLOR AFTER SUPPER, Baxter took his usual seat near the window. He wanted to be near Miss Kensington, but when she smiled at Hayes, Baxter took a step back to survey the situation. He didn't want to put Miss Kensington into having to choose between suitors, not if she truly cared for Hayes.

"Baxter?" Gilbert pulled a chair close to where Baxter sat pretending to read while he stole glances at the object of his affections.

"Yes?"

"May I make an observation?"

"Certainly."

"You seem preoccupied by Miss Kensington. Is there any reason in particular?"

"I am her guardian while Mr. Kensington is away. It is my duty to keep her safe."

Gilbert glared at him with the perceptiveness of a vicar. "From whom are you protecting her? Mr. Hayes?"

"Yes."

Gilbert scoffed. "I knew you were still in denial."

Offended by his younger brother's assumptions, Baxter tried not to react too boldly as it would only prove his brother correct. "You know absolutely nothing."

"I may know a bit more than my eldest brother."

Baxter adjusted in his chair. Had he been so obvious? He was certain the only people who knew about the snowball fight were Gigi and Phineas. Neither of them would have outted him. "What are you going on about?"

"You have developed a preference for Miss Kensington, more so than any other woman of our acquaintance, and it frightens you that she might not return your feelings."

"You are speaking nonsense."

"I can see fear in your eyes."

Baxter turned his head away, so his brother couldn't see the vulnerability in his expression. Gilbert had always been too perceptive, which was one reason he made a good vicar. "Keep your insights and sermonizing for the congregation."

"Why will you not admit your preference for Miss Kensington? We have all noticed it."

"What?" Baxter tried to whisper, but his outburst caused everyone in the room to stop speaking and look in their direction. Baxter ignored them and lowered his voice further. "What have you noticed?"

Gilbert chuckled. "Where should I begin?"

"Do not try my patience, brother." Baxter's growl was intended to intimidate. Instead, it caused Gilbert to double over in laughter. "I am losing my resolve to stay calm."

"Well, if that is the case," Gilbert said with mock sincerity, "then I shall have to comply with your request."

"Go on."

"You have despised Mr. Hayes from the moment he first noticed Miss Kensington."

Baxter could easily shrug off this accusation. "Mr. Hayes is a contradiction I have yet to understand. I have decided I do not care for him because I find his actions to be a counterfeit of his true nature."

"Very well," Gilbert said, conceding the point. "I think you enjoy sparring with Miss Kensington. You find her quick wit to be her most attractive feature."

"The woman drives me to insanity. How you could have come to such a conclusion, I will never know." Baxter sat back in his seat, no longer worried over his brother's interpretation of his emotions. Gilbert knew absolutely nothing. But even as he claimed she made him insane, he regretted it with a fierce intensity. He only hoped she would never discover the content of his current conversation.

"She has never cowered to your position, nor has she flaunted herself before you to ensnare you into an engagement. This above all else has caused you to take notice of her."

"I admit you are correct on one of your observations. Miss Kensington has certainly never tried to cause a scandal with me. It is one of her more refreshing characteristics. It would be terribly uncomfortable if she had tried."

"Finally, you watch her when you think no one notices."

Baxter was affronted by this accusation. It was a true statement, but he didn't like the way Gilbert made it sound. He didn't have nefarious reasons for watching Miss Kensington. "I most certainly do not. You make me sound like a filthy old man."

"You do. I am not the only one who has noticed. Archie, Fletch, and Gigi think you are in love with Miss Kensington. If you are not careful, Miss Kensington will take notice."

"If I were in love with Miss Kensington, it would be wrong of me to act upon my feelings. She is here as my guest until her grandfather returns. I cannot do anything to jeopardize her safety or her reputation."

"Courting her would not injure her reputation."

"It would be inappropriate while she is under my protection."

Gilbert leaned closer to Baxter, lowering his voice further. "Then transfer the duty to Archie or me."

Baxter narrowed his eyes at his brother. "If you were correct about my feelings, I would consider the possibility of doing so. But you are wrong. My interest is solely her welfare."

"Then you will not mind if Hayes asks for her hand in marriage?"

The possibility had always been in the forefront of Baxter's mind ever since Hayes had started pursuing Miss Kensington in earnest, but for his brother to ask such a pointed question so soon after Gigi had also made mention of it left Baxter short of breath. Instead of responding, Baxter stood and left the parlor, his mood completely changed back to the melancholy he'd known for so long.

Chapter Twenty-Five

With another sunny day ahead of her, Briar again spent her day out-of-doors. She hoped spring would arrive early, which might bring her grandfather back. Since her conversation with Lord Grafton the previous day, she'd hoped they would start speaking more often, but she feared it wasn't possible after he'd left the room so abruptly the night before.

His gloomy mood, and the hurried conversation with Gilbert left her wondering if Lord Grafton had the ability to be happy longer than a few minutes at a time. She'd seen pockets of joy within him, but every situation ended with him leaving the room to spend his time alone.

Having enjoyed the previous day at the bridge, Briar set out from Primrose Hall hoping to enjoy an afternoon in much the same way. As she neared the still frozen bridge, she was surprised to find Lord Grafton leaning on his elbows looking out at the same view she'd enjoyed the day before.

"Lord Grafton." Briar curtsied and tried not to sound too startled at his presence.

"Miss Kensington. I did not realize you knew how to find this place."

"I was here yesterday. I hoped to spend more time in the silence. But if you would prefer, I can leave."

Lord Grafton shook his head. "No. Please stay."

"Do you come here often?" She'd thought his haunts were the ruins and the cemetery. To find he enjoyed the bridge as well left her wondering if there were a place in Yorkshire he didn't visit.

"It isn't as dangerous as the ruins as the snow melts, so I spend a little bit of my time here in the winter. The bridge is hidden within the trees, and so I did not expect you to know of it."

Briar wanted to spend more time with Lord Grafton, but she feared it would only cause more heartache. She was convinced there would never be anything more than a possible friendship between them, and so it was wrong to hope for more.

"Miss Kensington, you look like you could use a confidant. As your protector, I have the duty of listening to your concerns."

She wondered if it was wise to tell him of Mr. Hayes's proposal. If she did, and Hayes hadn't received permission to make the offer, would it cause a rift between them? Every part of her wanted to share her concerns with Lord Grafton, especially now that she knew she admired him.

Briar raised her eyebrows and hoped the confession she was about to make would stay between them. His honesty made her think vulnerability was the right course. "You are certain you wish me to confide in you?"

"Yes."

His answer came so swiftly she was certain he would keep her confidence, and so she continued with the confession. "I came here yesterday in hopes of working through some difficult decisions."

"Were you able to resolve your concerns?"

"Yes, at least I have made a decision on how to proceed. Mr. Hayes has asked for my hand in marriage, and I needed time to consider everything that would entail. I had much to consider, given he has made a pointed effort at courting me." She'd looked past Lord Grafton once the confession was made, unwilling to know what his reaction was. If he was glad that she didn't want to marry Mr. Hayes, it would give her hope of a future with the earl. If he was upset over her continued presence in his home, she would have to accept Hayes, even if she didn't want to marry him and free Lord Grafton from his position as her protector. More than that, if he was unhappy with her decision, her heart wouldn't be able to handle an outright rejection. While she still didn't know his feelings toward her, she could pretend there was something more to their relationship than protector and ward.

With his silence, she decided she would have to glance in his direction. Lord Grafton's easy welcoming manner had turned cold, much like he'd been the first time she'd met him. Although the sun heated her face, a wave of ice ran through her body as Lord Grafton glared at her. "And you have decided to accept his proposal? I am your protector while your grandfather is away. Do you not think it appropriate to discuss the proposal with me before accepting?"

She had wanted to tell him her concerns and the reasons she would refuse Mr. Hayes, but Lord Grafton's displeasure at her confession left her baffled, which resulted in a flare of her temper. It wasn't either of the scenarios she'd imagined. "I do not have to answer to you. My grandfather will return before long, and I will share my decision with him."

"Then you have decided to marry Mr. Hayes?" Lord Grafton turned to face her, his hands on his hips and his glare as cold as the icy river below them.

"What concern is it to you?"

"I am your protector." Grafton's controlled anger left her questioning if the man had the ability to yell. He never raised his voice at her, but she always felt the sting of rebuke. "If you are engaged to Mr. Hayes, it would be my duty to have the banns posted."

She could have told him the truth; she didn't plan to accept Mr. Hayes's offer. But she was annoyed by his assumption. "Duty, is that all you ever think about?"

"If I do not conform to the demands of my title and station, I am nothing."

"Duty. Honor. Society. Those three words overlook the most important things in life." Briar hated every one of those words. She didn't want to marry a man who couldn't see past the expectations of people who didn't matter. "Feelings. Emotions. Love. Those are things that matter."

"I cannot expect an American to understand. The Colonist Uprising is enough evidence to show you have no idea what honor is."

Briar wanted to scream. Words didn't matter. She wanted to express her frustration without tears, yet her traitorous emotions allowed a sob to escape her throat. She'd been foolish to believe Lord Grafton could ever love her. The life she'd imagined the previous day, where they could have a family and future together, quickly dissolved with his unbending assumptions.

She needed to get away from him before he realized she was crying. Unsettled by his rudeness, she walked to the end of the bridge and then realized Primrose Hall was in the opposite direction. She would have to recross and pass by the odious man again, but she refused. She didn't want to be near him. Instead, she looked to the frozen river and gingerly made her way down to the bank by stepping on the rocks along the declining ground.

"Miss Kensington, what are you doing?" The pounding of Lord Grafton's boots as he ran across the bridge encouraged Briar to increase her pace. She wouldn't give him the satisfaction of having an impact on how she crossed the river. She would do as she pleased. "Miss Kensington, please forgive me. I did not mean what I said."

Briar turned to look at the man who rarely had anything kind to say to her. She was tired of his accusations. With tears streaming down her face, pooling under her chin, Briar couldn't even offer a glare of disdain. She was hurt and she needed him to understand how his words had affected her. "I am not to blame for the Revolutionary War. I was not alive when the Colonists revolted, and I have never handled a weapon. I did not cause your precious King George III to lose his mind. And I do not want to marry Mr. Hayes. I simply want to go home."

She hadn't realized until that moment how much she wanted to leave Yorkshire. Certainly, she missed her parents and she missed her home in Boston, but there had been times when she'd thought a life in England wouldn't be bad, not if she had her grandfather and people around her who loved her. But Lord Grafton and the Society he represented, with their unbending rules for perfection, left her empty. She would never fit into the mold they expected.

"There is ice on the rocks, and the thaw has started on the lake. It is too dangerous for you to cross beneath the bridge. Please, take my hand and I will help you back up the incline." Lord Grafton stood before her, making himself look like a gentleman, but she knew better than to believe the illusion before her. He'd presented himself with manners before, and then he'd proven it was all a show again and again.

"I am not a child, and I will do as I please." She closed her eyes in embarrassment as she realized her statement sounded reckless and childish.

"Miss Kensington, please do not put yourself in danger. I apologize for losing my temper, and I will expect you to abuse my character to everyone within Yorkshire and the surrounding areas, but please do not try to cross the river. The ice is not safe."

Briar ignored him and stretched forth her foot to test the ice. If the edge held her weight, the rest would be safe. As she gingerly placed her foot on the ice, it instantly shattered, and water flowed up through the cracks. Briar thought about running to the middle of the river where the ice would be thicker and still frozen, but her breath caught in her throat as the warmth of Lord Grafton's arms closed around her and pulled her to safety.

She didn't argue or fight against his hold, she simply allowed him to rescue her from her moment of reckless abandon. His touch opened a flood of fluttering through her body. Her mind went fuzzy as she looked into his eyes and her heart raced. But even with all of that, she felt empty. He'd saved her life. She was certain of it. Instead of offering her thanks, when he released her, Briar ran away from him. She couldn't look at him, not now that she knew there would never be a future for her in Yorkshire and in his life. She'd allowed herself to believe he could possibly care for her, and it had all ended in ruin.

Briar didn't stop running until she was certain Lord Grafton couldn't see her. She was embarrassed for her behavior and ashamed of the fanciful dreams she'd entertained the previous day. She wouldn't go back to Primrose Hall. She couldn't continue living under the protection of a man who couldn't see her as anything but an enemy.

Knowing she had nowhere to go other than a pretend home, Briar turned in the direction of Kensington Park. She would prefer to stay by herself instead of spending one more minute under the protection of Lord Grafton.

Chapter Twenty-Six

Baxter felt cold as he watched Miss Kensington run away. He'd lost his temper, again. But in his defense, the thought of Mr. Hayes as her husband had left Baxter ill. He couldn't lose her to a fop, and yet he had lost her. The speed at which she'd escaped his embrace left him reeling.

Pacing along the bank of the river, Baxter berated himself for overreacting. He should have listened to everything she said and allowed her to share her thoughts. He'd promised to be a confidant, and the minute she'd shared her secrets, he'd lost control. He was more than a fool. He'd proven to be the odious and ill-tempered wretch she'd accused him of being.

Knowing another apology was in order, Baxter walked in the direction of Primrose Hall. He would ask her forgiveness, and this time he would make her a solemn vow upon his honor to never lose his temper again.

Baxter ignored his surroundings as he marched with purpose toward his home. Water and mud splattered upon his boots as he took no care in avoiding the puddles along the path. As winter was slowly melting away, Baxter could see the eventual start of spring and the hope of a new beginning with budding flowers. It would be at least another month before they were fully out of winter, but he hoped it was a sign of what he could have with Briar.

"Baxter, you look a fright!" Gigi didn't hold back on her shock at his appearance. As Baxter took in the mud that had splashed up to his waist, he decided it didn't matter. He needed to clear the air with Miss Kensington before calling for his valet.

"Is Miss Kensington in the parlor?"

"No, she went for a walk and has yet to return."

He'd hoped to make his apologies with haste, and the continued delay felt unnecessary. "When do you think she will return?"

"I do not know. What has happened? You are out of sorts."

Baxter didn't want to confide in his mother. She didn't need to confirm her suspicions of his foolishness. "I do not care to speak of it. Will you send for me when she returns?"

Gigi stepped in his path, stopping him from leaving for his chambers. "Baxter, what happened?"

"Nothing of great significance." As he said the words, he pinched the bridge of his nose and closed his eyes to hide his guilty conscience.

"Baxter William Octavius Fernley, you will tell me this instant what you have done." It wasn't a threat but a demand. Gigi had used his entire given name, and he knew she would not relent.

"Did you know Hayes made an offer of marriage? I am her protector, and he did not request my blessing upon the match. Miss Kensington spent an entire day reviewing her decision, and yet she did not think it appropriate to let me know of the situation." Baxter noticed the lack of surprise from his mother. Narrowing his eyes in her direction, he saw the truth upon her face. "You knew about the offer."

"Yes, I did. He offered for her the morning of your snowball fight." Her lack of shame left Baxter speechless. He never would have entertained the possibility of a relationship with Miss Kensington without his mother's request. He would have ignored the growing desire within him and left her to court Mr. Hayes. Instead, his mother had encouraged the admiration.

"How could you keep this from me? After everything I shared with you, how could you leave me in the dark?" The betrayal from his mother hurt. He'd never thought her capable of keeping such an important secret.

"Briar requested the strictest confidence. I could not break my vow to her."

Baxter ran a hand through his hair, his confusion over Gigi's dedication to their guest baffled him. "I am your son."

"You will have to forgive me for the oversight, but I stand by my decision."

Knowing his mother would never apologize, Baxter decided he would prefer to be alone. He went to his bedchamber and removed his dirty, wet clothing, but instead of going to the general rooms in the house, he stayed in his chambers where he could spend the rest of his day in uncomfortable angst.

Miss Kensington had stolen his heart, his desire for order, and his sense of duty and honor. He no longer cared about his role as her protector. He would not lose her to Mr. Hayes, and to make certain he was the one to secure her hand in marriage, he would declare his love for her that very evening. If he had to make a spectacle of himself in front of his family, he would do so.

BAXTER WAS READY TO POUR HIS HEART OUT TO THE woman he loved. He'd spent the afternoon composing his speech and then memorizing every line he could think of to explain the way Miss Kensington made his heart pound. He would make certain she knew he would cease to exist if she was not his wife. For his offer of marriage, he would wear his blue waistcoat and black evening jacket. He had everything planned out, including her reaction.

He was certain upon hearing his confession of love, Miss Kensington would fall into his embrace and make her own declaration. All the arguing from that morning and the previous months would be forgotten. He would assign Archie to be Miss Kensington's protector, and they would send a letter to her grandfather.

Confident in his ability to secure Miss Kensington's hand in marriage, Baxter pulled the bell cord to summon his valet. It was time he dressed for the evening meal. As he walked to the corner of the room and reached for the cord, a knock sounded on his door.

"Enter."

Archie entered. Baxter noticed he had yet to dress for supper. "Baxter, do you know where Briar is?"

"No, I have been in here since I returned this morning." He'd purposefully stayed out of her way so she could calm down before he declared himself. The continued animosity between them needed to end.

"She never returned from her walk this morning. We plan to search for her."

Baxter didn't need to hear anymore. He would join his brothers and find Miss Kensington. Deep down, Baxter had an inkling he was the reason Miss Kensington hadn't returned to Primrose Hall. She had been upset when they'd last spoken. He realized it was possible that he'd offended her more than he'd realized.

Chapter Twenty-Seven

Kensington Park, Yorkshire, and England weren't her home. She'd tried to make the best out of her situation, but it was obvious no one would fully accept her into their lives. Perhaps Mr. Hayes would do so, but now having understood feelings of love, she couldn't accept marriage with merely a congenial friendship.

Lord Grafton had the ability to make her heart flutter with pure happiness. That was the man she'd fallen in love with. Unfortunately, when the odious earl made an appearance, she wished with all her heart that that part of the man she loved would go away.

Kensington Park was empty. Her grandfather must have sent the servants away while he was on the continent. Thankfully, the kitchen door had been unlocked allowing her the afternoon to pack her belongings. She would find her way back to the shipyard and purchase fare back to Boston. She was tired of living amongst the snobby elite of England.

Sitting at her writing desk, Briar lit a candle as the sun lowered in the sky. Her stomach made a gurgling sound, reminding her she hadn't eaten since the morning meal. But hunger was nothing to the need for the comfort of home. She had two last tasks before setting out for Boston. She needed to thank Gigi for her love and hospitality, and she needed to let her grandfather know where she'd gone.

The letters were difficult to write. With the emotions of her last argument fresh in her mind, Briar allowed tears to fall, blotching the ink and making most of what she wrote unreadable. With the swirl of her signature, Briar left both letters open on the table so the ink could dry.

There was no reason to be nostalgic about Kensington Park. Her father hadn't wanted to live in England, and she now understood his reasons. As the son of a merchant and a working man, he'd been considered an upstart and new money. He hadn't fit into the *ton*, and neither did she. With every part of her soul aching for acceptance, Briar held the lit candle in one hand and took hold of the handle on the end of her trunk and laboriously pulled it toward the door. The scraping of the trunk on the carpet left her wondering if it would rip a hole, but she shrugged off the concern as she knew her grandfather could afford to replace anything she ruined.

She would miss her grandfather, but she'd had practice while he'd been away. If he planned to travel like her father had, she would rarely see him. If she'd realized this, she would have chosen to stay in Boston instead of uprooting her life to live with family.

When she'd left Boston, her home had been vacant, a museum of her past. No matter how inappropriate, she would live there alone. She didn't need a companion or an escort. She had her parents' money. Encouraged with these thoughts, Briar dropped her trunk at the top of the stairs. She was out of breath and needed to rest before dragging her belongings to the main floor. Wiping the sweat from her forehead, Briar sat on the top step and buried her head in her hands.

Her plan would work, she was certain of it. Mumbling to herself, Briar voiced the thought plaguing her heart. "I will never see Lord Grafton again." With all the arguing they'd done, this should be a happy thought. But she was certain her heart would never heal. "How can I love such a vexing man?"

Unfortunately, no one was there to answer the question. She didn't have anyone to explain the emotions welling up inside her, and as she rested from pulling the trunk, she cried over the loss of what could have been.

"Briar?"

At the sound of Lord Grafton's voice, Briar sat up and instantly put her defenses back in place. She stood and picked up the end of her trunk again. She wouldn't give him the satisfaction of carrying it for her.

"What are you doing here?" Briar asked. She noticed the front door to Kensington Park was open. She'd tried the door earlier and it had been locked. "How did you get into the house?"

"Mr. Kensington gave me the key. I have secured the property while he is away."

Determined to leave the country, Briar started down the stairs. Her trunk hit the first step with an echoing thud. "Are you the one who sent the servants away?"

Lord Grafton shook his head. "No, your grandfather paid them for the quarter and offered them the time to spend with their families. No one will return until he is ready to come back."

"When is that?" She had a feeling he was more informed about her grandfather's plans than she was. "Does he ever plan to return?"

"Yes, of course he does. Briar, if you wanted your belongings, I could have sent your maid and a carriage to collect the items. You needn't have come on your own."

There were two issues ringing through her head. She would take care of both and then be on her way. "My lord, you do not have permission to use my Christian name, and I do not plan on returning to Primrose Hall. I have left a forwarding address for the belongings still at your home. I request you send them forthwith."

Lord Grafton's confusion would have made her laugh if he wasn't also distressed. "Where are you going?"

"Home."

Removing his hat and gloves, Lord Grafton took a moment before responding. She knew it was his way of gathering his thoughts. "Your home is Primrose Hall until Mr. Kensington returns."

She watched as Lord Grafton placed his hat on a table at the bottom of the steps and put his gloves inside it. With ease, he took hold of the banister and stood on the bottom step. She hadn't wanted a confrontation. She'd hoped to leave the country without notice.

"I do not belong in your home."

"Miss Kensington," Lord Grafton said as he slowly ascended the staircase, "if your decision is based on my abominable behavior this morning, I beg of you to reconsider. Please do not make a hasty decision that will be difficult to take back."

"The only decision I regret is asking you to keep my confidence. I should never have trusted you."

The pained look she'd come to associate with Lord Grafton crossed his face. He stopped a few steps below where she stood, keeping a proper distance. "I agree, my reaction to your confession this morning was unfounded. But, if you understood my reasons for behaving so abhorrently, you would forgive me, I am certain."

Briar wasn't in a forgiving mood. "Nothing you can say would make me forgive you. This is not the first time you have treated me ill."

She wasn't surprised when Lord Grafton put his hands on his hips, one foot placed on the step above where his other was planted. "You are correct. I have behaved terribly since our first meeting. But I dare say I am not the only one who has treated the other ill."

Affronted by his accusation, Briar dropped her trunk on the step where she stood, the resounding thud causing her to close her eyes and scrunch her face as it echoed through the empty halls of Kensington Park. She imitated Lord Grafton by putting her hands on her hips while glaring at the man. "I have only ever responded in kind to your rudeness. If you would have behaved like a gentleman, I would have been less confrontational."

She expected him to lose his temper. If he did, she would take hold of her trunk again and pull it down the stairs, pushing past him without delay. Instead, she stood rooted to the stairs in utter shock. "I owe you a thousand apologies and I plan to spend the rest of my life making amends for my loathsome behavior. Can we not make a solemn vow to listen when the other is speaking, instead of making accusations?"

The rest of his life? Was he in earnest? "There is no need, my lord. I do not plan to be in England long enough for you to concern yourself over me."

"What do you mean?"

"I am leaving for Boston this very minute."

Lord Grafton stepped up three more stairs leaving only two between them. "No, you are not. I will not allow it."

"You cannot stop me."

Lord Grafton's voice rose in a controlled frustration. "I am your protector. You cannot leave the country without my approval, and I most certainly do not agree to such a foolish voyage."

"I release you from the duty. I do not need a protector, and I do not need you."

Lord Grafton took another step up, leaving only one step between them. Her breath caught in her throat, and she knew arguing was futile. He believed duty was more important than homesickness.

"Miss Kensington, will you allow me to explain my reasons for losing my temper this morning?"

"Only if you agree to my decision to go home to Boston."

She didn't expect him to agree. She imagined he would drag her back to Primrose Hall and lock her in her bedchamber. "I agree. If my confession does not convince you to stay, I will personally escort you to Boston and ensure your well-being."

She stretched forth her hand to shake on the deal. Lord Grafton took it, but instead of clasping it as she'd expected, he placed a kiss on her knuckles. "This is unfair," Briar bemoaned.

"What is?"

"You cannot suddenly decide to behave like a gentleman. I am still far too angry with you to allow such pleasantries."

"Then why did you stretch forth your hand?"

"For the agreement. You were supposed to take it to strike a deal." It put a smile on her face to see him struggling with a retort. She knew exactly what he was holding back, and it softened her anger to know he was attempting to be kind. The odious earl would have commented about her uncultured ways, but the apologetic man in front of her was biting his tongue.

As he released his tightened jaw, Lord Grafton let only two words escape his mouth. "I see."

Briar adjusted her stance but kept a stern glare upon him. She still didn't trust him. "So, what is your pitiful excuse?"

"I cannot allow you to marry Mr. Hayes. When you told me he offered for your hand, I feared you had accepted."

Briar interrupted his speech, but only because she was still in an argumentative mood. "I never said I accepted. I wanted you to know I planned to refuse his offer, and since my grandfather made you my protector, I needed your support."

"I realize this now. But when I thought I had lost you, my defenses went up, and I was hurt."

"Whatever for?" Briar folded her arms across her body. She hadn't heard anything to make her want to stay in Yorkshire. Her mind was set upon Boston, and she would not yield.

Lord Grafton's posture straightened. With his head held high, he let out an exasperated sigh before answering. "Miss Kensington, I am in love with you, and the reality of another man taking you as his wife was too much for me to bear and so I lashed out. It was easier to mask my pain than it was to beg you to consider me."

The hope of love was before her. All she had to do was tell him she felt the same, but she couldn't. The ache for home and belonging wouldn't go away because a handsome man had declared his love. She wanted to fall into his arms, but home beckoned, and so she stopped herself from making any confessions.

"Thank you for the kind words. But I would prefer to go home." Her voice cracked as she said the word home. More than anything, she wanted to belong somewhere, and she feared it would only happen in Boston. There was nothing for her in England.

Lord Grafton's eyes went wide, and his face contorted in pain. "Please reconsider."

She didn't know much about the upper crust of British Society, but she was certain earls didn't beg granddaughters of merchants. A pang of sorrow pierced her heart and a heaviness built up in her chest, but she would not stray from her current course. "I do not belong here."

"Then neither do I."

"How absurd!" Briar would not be manipulated into staying where she wasn't wanted. "You are a staple of Society. As earl and magistrate, the people depend upon your wisdom. Everyone loves you."

"Everyone, except you." His words cut through her, and Briar wanted to take every awful word she'd ever said and replace it with something kind. Did he truly love her? Could he love someone he thought so ill-bred and unfit for his Society? Lord Grafton reached forward and lifted her trunk. "I will make arrangements to return you to Boston."

Briar slowly followed him out of the house. He'd respected her wishes, which was much more than she'd done for him. He'd declared himself in love, and she'd kept her true feelings hidden. The people around her moved about, her trunk was handed off to a footman, Gilbert stood by a carriage, and Lord Grafton patiently waited for her to accept his hand. This time it wasn't in marriage, but to help her step into the waiting carriage.

As the door to the carriage closed and it pitched forward with a jerk, Briar shyly investigated the face of the man who had stolen her heart. Did she love him enough to stay in England? Would his admiration and a life with him fulfill the ache within her soul?

The confused pain she'd noticed so many times was frozen on his face, and she didn't like it. She'd originally thought he was a cruel man, but during her time at Primrose Hall, she'd found him to be a man who spent time serving the people, and it wasn't out of a sense of duty and his title, it was because he genuinely cared for others.

She'd refused his love. He hadn't offered marriage, not in the same way Mr. Hayes had done. Lord Grafton had offered love, and she had turned him away. He'd declared himself more fully than any man had ever done, and she decided it wasn't fair. A man didn't have the right to be so odious and lovely within the same day. Gathering her courage, Briar decided their conversation hadn't ended.

She didn't care that Gilbert sat in the carriage with them. He would have to ignore the conversation or pretend to not hear if his vicarly sensibilities were offended by her confession. Thankful the candlelight on the outside of the carriage shone directly upon Lord Grafton's face, Briar looked to the man she hoped would forgive her unkind words. Briar didn't hold back. He deserved her censure, but he also deserved a confirmation that his feelings were returned. "How dare you treat me with disdain in the morning and then declare your love for me hours later. What did you expect me to do, burst into tears and fall into your embrace?"

"Can we speak about this later?" Lord Grafton growled. His voice was strained with embarrassment.

"I had a perfectly good plan to return to my home in Boston and leave this horrible place behind, and you had to ruin everything by claiming to love me."

"What would you like me to say?"

"Apologize for ruining my plans."

"I will not apologize for declaring myself to you. You should apologize for treating my declaration with disdain."

Briar held to the side of the carriage as the wheel went into a hole, jostling everyone within. She regretted the cruel way she had rejected his feelings for her. When Mr. Hayes had asked for her hand, she hadn't refused him outright, instead she'd told him she needed time. Why had she not done the same for Lord Grafton? Why had she denied the flutter of joy his words had brought to her stomach? "If you had meant the words you said, then I might have been more appreciative."

Lord Grafton visibly sighed. "A man does not say such things as a jest. I meant every word."

Briar knew her cheeks were pink, and she didn't mind. He needed to see her blush to know exactly how she felt. If she didn't fix the situation, it was possible he'd arrange her passage on a ship and send her back to Boston, and the thought of losing Lord Grafton made her want to sob. She tried to sound smug, and even put her nose in the air as she prepared to say the most scandalous thing she'd ever considered, but she was desperate.

"An earnest declaration would have included a kiss."

The ensuing silence told her she'd gone too far. Lord Grafton would be right to send her to the local coaching inn while he arranged transportation to the docks. The only reason she wasn't hiding her face in the fabric of the blanket covering her legs was because she hoped he would understand she was accepting his offer of love and then ask for her hand.

As the carriage hit another hole, Briar tightened her grip to stay upright. Holes with water were joyful when hopping in them, but not when riding in a carriage, even one as well sprung as Earl Grafton's. She waited for Lord Grafton's response.

"You are right, Miss Kensington, I should have done a proper job of it. It was an oversight on my part, and if you will allow me to make amends, I will do so with haste."

"I should say it would be appropriate. You would not want the gossips in town to hear about your—" Briar stopped speaking as Lord Grafton hastily switched to her side of the carriage. He sat next to her; his eyes focused upon her lips. Picking up where she'd left off, Briar tried to remember what she had been saying. His nearness left her out of sorts. "The gossips would put you to shame if they knew you had only kissed my hand upon such an offering." She couldn't remember if that was all she wanted to say. Was she marring the moment with her incessant chatter?

His gaze pulled her toward him. Briar closed the gap by leaning into him, and when he claimed her lips, she eagerly returned his kiss with every part of her soul humming in delight.

Lord Grafton pulled away as Gilbert let out an exaggerated cough. "Don't mind me."

Growling at his brother, Lord Grafton's smile lit up his face. "Can you not think of a hymn or scriptures to review while you sit quietly in the corner?"

"I was actually going to ask: would you prefer I post the banns or send for a special license?"

Briar sat comfortably in the crook of Lord Grafton's arm realizing the peace she'd associated with her parents and Boston was now resting upon her soul. Home wasn't a place, and love wasn't found within the walls of a building or upon the shores of a country. Everything she'd been searching for was currently holding her in his arms.

Chapter Twenty-Eight

The evening couldn't have been better. When Lord Grafton had announced their engagement, he'd done so while holding her hands. Gone were his stiff unbending mannerisms. They'd been replaced with a light bounce in his step and a silly grin when he gazed at her. When Gigi embraced her, Briar knew she'd always be a part of the family. She had made the right decision to accept Lord Grafton and stay in England. She would consider Primrose Hall her home, forever.

As she lay in bed reviewing her day, she'd never expected it to end so wonderfully. She would soon be Lady Grafton, upon receiving her grandfather's approval, and all would be perfect.

Rolling to her side, Briar had a nagging feeling her inward declaration of perfection was not exactly achieved. She knew there was something she hadn't yet done. Going over everything from the day, Briar realized she hadn't disposed of the letters sitting on her writing desk at Kensington Park. Since she was no longer leaving for Boston, she would have to retrieve them and throw them in the fire.

Settling deeper into her soft pillow and warm bed, the nagging thought continued to plague her. "What have I forgotten?" Briar asked to the dark room. There was no one to answer her and save her the distress of an absent memory. Rolling to her back, she looked up at the canopy of yellow silk bed curtains while she reviewed her day. "I ate the morning meal and then I took a walk out to the bridge where I fought with Lord Grafton." As she thought his name, his beautiful blue eyes entered her mind, and she took a moment to sigh over the contentment within her soul. She was engaged to Lord Grafton. "I will have to start referring to him as Baxter."

She liked the name, Baxter. "Baxter and Briar Fernley. I do like connecting our names. It is much better than..." Briar stopped speaking; did she know Mr. Hayes's first name? With the thought, she remembered what it was she had forgotten. "I have to speak with Mr. Hayes."

She hadn't formally refused his offer of marriage and would need to do so with urgency. If word of her engagement to Lord Grafton spread throughout Yorkshire Society, Mr. Hayes would be the first to hear of it.

She spent her night in angst, tossing and turning until the early hours of the morning. There was no way to soften the rejection. She would simply tell Mr. Hayes her answer was no and inform him of her decision to marry Lord Grafton. She hoped he would understand.

Mr. Hayes was far too punctual. It hadn't ever bothered her until she arrived for the morning meal to find him sitting next to Archie in a silent and tense dining room. Since everyone, including the staff, knew of her engagement to Lord Grafton, it was imperative she inform Mr. Hayes forthwith.

At her arrival, the men stood, as was customary. Briar quickly threw fruit on a plate and took her usual seat between Lord Grafton and Gigi. She smiled as a greeting, not trusting her voice to stay calm.

"Miss Kensington, I was telling Archie and Phineas about the latest news from London. I can start over if you would like to hear it." Mr. Hayes had a plate full of food that looked untouched. She wasn't surprised as he usually spent more time talking instead of eating.

"No thank you, Mr. Hayes."

"Do not worry, I will save the best part of my story for when we take a stroll. It is a beautiful morning. I do not think it will be long before we can claim it is spring."

Briar closed her eyes to calm herself. Her heart was near to pounding out of her chest. Mr. Hayes, despite his eccentricities, was a good man. He didn't deserve to be treated so coldly. She berated herself for not refusing him immediately. She hadn't had trouble treating Lord Grafton with disdain, but that was because he'd made it so easy.

"Lord Grafton," Hayes continued speaking unaware of the tense silence around him, "do you know when Mr. Kensington will be back from France? I have a particular question I would like to ask him. If it will not be soon, I suppose since you are Miss Kensington's protector, I could gain your permission."

Briar couldn't handle it any longer. She stood, her chair scraping against the floor. She would have laughed at the ensuing rise of the men at the table, if it wasn't for the serious situation she was in and the pounding of her heart. She was certain the beating in her ears was audible to all. She wished the entire situation could be discussed in that room, but it was improper, and she wasn't a heathen.

"Mr. Hayes, I think we should take the air." She turned to see a maid standing in the corner. She didn't know the maid's name, nor did she care. She waved the stunned girl over. "You will come with us?"

"Yes, miss." The maid rushed to follow Briar out of the room.

Briar didn't look back at Lord Grafton, afraid she would see his displeasure. She knew he would gladly speak to Mr. Hayes, but this was her duty, and she would delay no longer. Ames opened the dining room door as she rushed to it, and he stayed ahead of her as she marched toward the front of the house where he held her bonnet, pelisse, and gloves. She was out the door before Mr. Hayes had situated his outerwear and primped himself in the looking glass.

She didn't plan to go far from the house, especially because the maid didn't have a covering. Seeing the discomfort she'd caused the poor girl; Briar removed her pelisse and forced the maid to take it by placing it on the girl's shoulders. The chilly morning air would make her speak faster, and the entire situation would be over with haste. Turning to Mr. Hayes, she could see he understood what she planned to say.

Mr. Hayes held up a hand to stop her from speaking. "You do not need to refuse my offer. I will withdraw it."

This was a surprise. "Pardon me?"

"It is obvious you and I will not suit. I will always be thankful we had this time together, and I will bid you farewell."

Briar looked to the maid and then back to the man before her. She'd expected more. As she stood in stunned disbelief, she wondered why it was so difficult to have Mr. Hayes withdraw his offer. She didn't want to marry him, so why did his words injure her feelings? Hesitating with her answer, Briar looked at the man and cautiously replied, "Thank you, Mr. Hayes."

Without another word, Mr. Hayes crossed the yard to his horse. His bright yellow pantaloons reflected the rays from the sun into her eyes. Confused, Briar looked to the maid and let out a sigh of relief. "That was much easier than I thought it would be."

"I am happy for you, miss."

Briar walked back into the house and deposited her outerwear into Ames's outstretched arms. "Thank you, Ames."

"You are very welcome, miss."

Briar was too embarrassed to go back into the dining room, so she made her way to the library, knowing Lord Grafton would find her there. Briar sat in the window seat, looking out at the beauty of the world. Hayes had been right when he'd said spring was on the way. The snow had almost completely melted, and although it was still very wet, it wouldn't be long before they could spend their days out of doors.

If her grandfather returned from France, she and Lord Grafton could marry amongst blossoming trees, spring flowers, and chirping birds. She considered marrying Lord Grafton in the church house, but her heart ached for their union to happen in the place where she had realized he was a better man than she'd given him credit. The ruins would always be a special place for them, and she hoped he would agree to the outdoor wedding.

"How long have you been in here?" Lord Grafton's voice broke through her planning.

"Not long. I was waiting for you."

Lord Grafton crossed the room and sat next to her in the window box. "How did your conversation with Mr. Hayes go? Did he understand?"

"I did not have to say anything. He realized I was ready to refuse him, and so he chose to back out of the offer."

"He did what?" Lord Grafton stood and paced the room, his hand running through his hair. "He is fully aware of the impropriety of such an action. Did anyone know he offered for your hand?"

Briar shook her head. "Only your family, as far as I am aware. Lord Grafton, why does this bother you?"

Lord Grafton stopped and turned to her. "You must never use my title again. Please call me Baxter."

"Of course." She knew there wasn't a need to permit him to use her Christian name. He had used it the previous day without shame.

"Briar, if Hayes tells anyone he chose to end an offer of marriage, you could be ruined."

"I suppose you will have to marry me before my reputation suffers." Briar hadn't meant her statement to sound so wanton, and she blushed furiously when Baxter raised his eyebrows, clearly scandalized.

"Then you would prefer the special license?" Baxter asked as he pulled her into his arms.

"Yes, especially because I do not want to be married in the church house."

"Then where? Primrose Hall?"

Briar shook her head. "Baxter, I want to become your wife in the most beautiful place Yorkshire has to offer."

"The ruins."

Briar didn't have a chance to confirm his guess as he leaned in and once again claimed her lips. She wrapped her arms around his neck, pulling him closer. She didn't want him to pull away before they had both agreed they were finished kissing.

Chapter Twenty-Nine

Baxter sat across from his six brothers, each looking at him with concern. He didn't blame them. He'd spent more than enough time worrying over their futures, but he'd never considered whether any of them gave him a second thought.

Gilbert, as the spiritual advisor for their family, took the lead. "Baxter, we are aware of Briar's finer qualities. She is well-bred, kind, genuine, and an heiress. These are all qualities men in your position require. But our concern is the lack of mutual affection. Since the day you met her, there has been a distinct animosity between you."

Archibald nodded and added his observations. "Do not misunderstand us, we have all grown in accord with Briar and consider her a sister, but none of us thought you would marry her."

Gilbert held up a hand to stop the others from jumping into the conversation. "Archie is attempting to help you understand the confusion we feel over this announcement. We thought Briar was a better match for Oliver."

It was true Briar and Oliver had spent time together as he instructed her on the flute. Baxter hadn't considered them a match.

Looking to his youngest brother, Baxter worried he'd injured Oliver with his announcement.

"I was unaware of your feelings for Briar. I thought you considered her a friend or sister. Do you prefer her above all other women?" Baxter wasn't prepared to hear his brother's answer. If Oliver was in love with Briar, it could cause a rift in their family. He had to ask himself, if Oliver did love Briar, whether could he sacrifice his own happiness for his youngest brother.

"Do not concern yourself with my feelings. Briar and I have developed a lasting friendship, and she refused my offer weeks ago."

Cornelius cleared his throat. "You offered marriage? Why did you not tell any of us?"

Baxter's angst rose as Oliver's face went pale. The truth of Cornelius's statement hung in the silence. Unable to look at his brothers, Baxter stared at one of the walls that was covered in books. He knew the subject matter on those shelves was science ranging from astronomy to zoology. His father and the earls before him had built up a collection of books worth pursuing when one had free time. Baxter would give anything to be looking at a book on botany instead of discussing the possibility of his younger brother being in love with his intended.

"There was nothing to mention. Briar and I agreed to stay friends, and I will not only wish Briar joy, but I hope with all my heart that my eldest brother will have a full and happy marriage."

Gilbert shook his head, obviously not believing a word Oliver said. "We have seen you and Briar together over the past month. You are not being honest."

"Gilbert, you were in the carriage with Baxter and Briar. Did she accept his offer of marriage?" Oliver's question lent merit and consideration.

"Yes."

"Then what I do or do not feel has no bearing on this conversation. If Briar accepted Baxter's offer, then they are engaged, and that is the end of it."

Baxter quietly corrected his brother. "The beginning." This engagement and eventual marriage would be the beginning of his life with Briar and their future family.

Gilbert looked to his twin brother for support. "Phineas, what do you have to say about this?"

"Baxter has the prior claim to Briar's affection, I am certain of it. She is friendly with each of us, but she is in love with Baxter. I saw it when he hit her with the snowball. It was the first time she'd allowed herself to laugh around Baxter, and I knew then that they would be a good match."

Not getting the response he wanted, Gilbert turned to Fletcher. "What do you have to say about this?"

Baxter was tired of the conversation. Instead of allowing any further comments, he interrupted anything Fletcher would have said. "Gilbert, you were in the carriage when Briar and I reconciled our differences. I cannot in good conscience allow her to marry anyone else."

He'd kissed her, passionately, in front of his brother who also happened to be the local vicar. Even Gilbert had made the observation that a special license would be best. Once Baxter had the approval of Mr. Kensington, he planned to marry Briar.

Baxter continued speaking. "For now, Archie will take my place as her protector, and I will send a messenger to France in the morning." Baxter stood, indicating the conversation was over. But he did look to his younger brother. "I am sorry, Oliver. I will be more attentive in the future. Trust me when I tell you I will never steal another woman's affections away from you."

As his brothers left him alone, Baxter took his seat once more and stared back at the wall of books. He understood how Oliver could have fallen for Briar, but attraction and love were two different emotions. If Oliver were truly in love with Briar, he would have reacted with anger over the engagement, but it didn't stop Baxter from adding this to his list of concerns for his family. He would keep an eye on Oliver and make certain his youngest brother didn't wallow in heartbreak over losing Briar.

As Baxter joined the family for afternoon tea, he was amazed at the overwhelming love within him for Briar. Now that he'd allowed himself to declare his admiration, it was easier to be near her. Instead of sitting by the window, Baxter sat on the sofa next to Briar. She poured his tea and handed him a plate with assorted sweets.

He no longer had a desire to vex her, and she seemed to have lost the will to argue with everything he said. He hoped what they felt in that moment would stay forever part of their relationship and never be broken.

Gigi either didn't know about the conversation Baxter had suffered through with his brothers, or she didn't agree with them. She took hold of his hand, and with her words, she stilled all the concerns Baxter had for Oliver. "I do not have the words to express how happy I am for Baxter and Briar. I knew from the moment I first met Briar that she and Baxter were a perfect match. I only hope each of my sons will find the right woman who will drive him to insanity and then bring them back from the brink of madness to realize it is truly love."

Baxter couldn't stop smiling. Gigi was right. Briar had made him question everything about himself and his duty. He'd often wondered if she could show any compassion, and now he knew it had all been worth the hours pacing in the library or sitting in the freezing cold at the ruins. He'd discovered that love was worth bending a few rules and honor could be found in many ways. Most importantly, she'd brought his best qualities out and had helped him find himself as an earl.

Epilogue

The snow had completely melted, leaving the lush green fields around Primrose Hall covered in beds of wildflowers with varying shades of purple, pink, yellow, and blue. Briar was certain no other place on earth had ever been so lovely. She'd chosen to be married as the sun rose in the sky, symbolizing the start of a new life, one that they could build together.

The wedding party had spent most of the day at the ruins, enjoying the peaceful ancient edifice. The ruins would forever stand in her mind as the place where her dreams became a reality. Although the brick was slowly decaying and bits continued to break and litter the earth beneath her feet, Briar planned to bring her future children to the place and allow them to build memories, much like she was doing with Baxter.

"Thank you for agreeing to hold the ceremony here." Briar laid her head against Baxter's shoulder as they sat on the topmost wall overlooking Primrose Hall and the surrounding estate and town.

"I could not bring myself to deny you anything, not after you agreed to marry such an odious man."

Briar laughed. "I suppose you considered it a request from the eccentric American."

Baxter kissed the top of her head and tightened his hold on her waist. "I hope you will one day forget the terrible comments I made during my bouts of poor manners."

"Never, for I could no sooner forget the love I feel for you."

"I certainly would not want that to happen."

"When did you know you were in love with me?"

Baxter took a moment before he responded. She appreciated this attribute of his personality. He never jumped to conclusions, jealous assumptions aside. "The morning we first met, when I saw your skirts were covered in mud, I knew I had met the most intriguing woman of my acquaintance. But it wasn't until you lay in the snow here at the ruins making a snow angel that I knew the fluttering in my heart and the unending thoughts penetrating every hour both waking and sleeping were those of love. It was here amongst the peaceful eroding ruins of my ancestors that I realized you were the only woman I could ever spend the rest of my life with."

He'd said everything she'd ever wanted to hear and more. Baxter had a way of declaring his love that left her breathless. She could not adequately explain how she'd spent months dreaming of his blue eyes and wishing he could see her as more than an enemy. Now that her life seemed perfect, she could rest in his loving embrace while looking out at the life they would build together.

Note from the Author

Thank you for taking the time to read *Earl Grafton and the Traitor*. The character of Baxter reached into my soul and pulled out some of my pain and insecurities of having lost a member of my family too soon and the fear of losing those still alive.

I have learned that the pain of loss never truly leaves us. It becomes a part of who we are and molds us into who we are supposed to become.

If you enjoyed this book and wish to leave a review, please do so on your favorite review sites. Reviews help authors sell books and they give the author encouragement to keep writing.

ANGELA

About the Author

Angela Johnson is an award winning editor of the 2021 Colorado Book Awards for her work on the publication *Monsters, Movies &* *Mayhem*. She has a love of literature and all things Regency. Traveling and reading are favorite past times and help her form ideas for writing. Angela despises the snow when it is on the road, but loves snow when it falls romantically in the perfect scene for characters to fall in love.

Follow Angela for book updates:
www.angelajohnsonauthor.org

Also by Angela Johnson

Earls of England Series

The Earl of Arundel

Saved by Scandal

Restoring Ashford Manor

An Assignation to Remember Series

Wit & Intrigue

Unmasking a Lady

Maid in the Stars

Fernley Family a Regency-era Romance

Earl Grafton and the Traitor

Mr. Fernley and the Lady

The Archaeologist and the Spinster

The Vicar and the Thief